RIDE THE DESPERATE TRAIL

MIKE KEARBY

Trail's End Books

Inquiries should be addressed to

Trails End Books
P.O. Box 201385
Austin, Texas 78720-1385

FIRST EDITION
First Printing 2007
Second Printing 2007

Publisher's Cataloging-in-Publication Data

1. Cowboy—Fiction 2. African-American—Fiction
3. Native American—Fiction 4. Texas History—Fiction

PS 3536 K319 2006 FIC Kea 2006910644

ISBN 978-0-9788422-7-7

Cover Design: Rebecca Duncan

While the *Ride the Desperate Trail* contains historical characters and events, the book is a work of fiction. All fictional characters and *all* of the dialogue are from the writer's imagination.

Trail's End
Books

Printed in the United States of America
at Morgan Printing in Austin, Texas

For: Kendra; who always makes me laugh.

No Man Can Escape His Own Times.

— Unknown

AUTHOR'S NOTE
RIDE THE DESPERATE TRAIL

As the first words of *Ride the Desperate Trail* scrolled across my computer screen, I knew most readers would see it as just another Western. Neverthe-less, from day one the novel was always about the clash of cultures on the Western frontier.

The societal roles of native peoples and settlers, both dis-tinct in their learned view of the world, played out day after day on the prairies of Texas, with each side willing to fight to the death for their cultural "right".

The quote "No man can escape his own times" became the major theme of the novel and all the characters in the book face a *yes* or *no* decision to continue their societal dictated roles.

Once I established the theme, the conflict of revenge gal-vanized within the culturally learned roles of each character. These roles were further conflicted by cultural differences inside each homogeneous group.

Would any of the characters "escape their times" or would they simply continue to play out their assigned roles? It was my hope that these questions would make the novel an inter-esting read.

I hope the readers think so too.

1. Anderson Homestead
2. The Flats
3. Fort Concho
4. Good Homestead
5. Agua de Mesteno
6. Lost Creek
7. The Sand Hills
8. Apache Seep
9. Old Pinery Station
10. Guadalupe Mountains
11. El Paso del Rio del Norte
12. Apache Winter Camp — Cañon de Sierra Carmel

RIDE THE DESPERATE TRAIL
Map 1868 – 1869

PROLOGUE

Mestizo's, Outside Fort Concho, Texas
November 1868

The lone rider eyed the three cavalry mounts tied to the split mesquite rail outside of Mestizo's. The man's face, hardened by a lifetime of weather and difficulty, appeared dangerous and uncaring. He cast a glance skyward, incensed by the humidity from a thunderstorm now pushed to the east. The nauseous heat pressed hard on every living thing and infuriated even the most gentle of souls.

The man dismounted and removed the salt-stained blackened hat from his forehead revealing a full head of golden hair. He pulled the bandana from his neck and wiped a bead of sweat from his brow. Deliberately, he tied his horse next to the cavalry mounts and examined the U.S.-issued property with a measured gaze. Each saddle carried the mark of the 10th Cavalry, Buffalo Soldiers. He stared at the horses, narrowed his eyes, and pulled his mouth taut. With little regard for the steeds' owners, he spat a glob of tobacco across the saddle of the nearest animal.

He tred up the three steps to the small way station. The sign on the door read *Bebida y Mecancías*. The robust merrymaking of dancing and women's voices blasted from inside. *Fiesta*, he thought.

Glancing back to his horse, he stared across the river toward Fort Concho. His eyes scanned the post for movement as his right hand instinctively tapped the pearl Colt handle jutting from his holster. He turned back in sullen disapproval, thrust the door open, and walked into the darkened bar.

CHAPTER 1

Anderson Homestead, Texas December 1868

A harsh wind blew cold on Free Anderson's cheek. Gray winter clouds, framed against a purple back drop hung low on the northern horizon forming a wall from north to east. Overnight a blue norther had gushed in, plummeting temperatures by forty degrees, a reminder to man and beast alike of the sudden changes common on the West Texas plains.

Free stood in the decay of the ancient abandoned Comanche Reservation near the Clear Fork of the Brazos. The numerous structures of a decade ago now sat in ruins. On the surrounding prairie, large rectangular piles of limestone jutted from the ground, giving a fort-like appearance to the landscape. Here, at the junction of the southern prairie and the river woodlands, the fertile plain teemed with deer, wild turkey, and waterfowl. And it was at this place that Free staked claim to his homestead.

Free and Parks looked over the recently constructed three-room house that rose majestically from the prairie. The men had built the structure from the drop logs that once formed the reservation agent's building and the readily available prairie limestone.

Free, an ex-Missouri slave, clapped his hands together and looked on with pride at their craftsmanship. "I never thought I'd see this day," he told his Civil War lieutenant and best friend.

"It's a fine home, Free," Parks said, "It's a home in which a man can raise a family."

Free turned back to the newly constructed corral and placed a loop of string around the corner post. He then turned and gave an OK signal to Parks.

The lieutenant secured his end over the opposite corner post and marked the string. "Appears to be square, Free."

Free walked toward his friend, the collar of his wool coat turned up and wrapped around his neck and ears. Great puffs of steam exited his mouth with each step. "Gosh, it's cold out here!"

Parks cupped his hands over his mouth and blew heated breath into them. "And by the looks of that cloud bank, this might set with us awhile."

"Well, thank goodness the corral is finished."

"Amen," Parks answered.

"Free! You two best come in and take your breakfast!"

Free glanced toward the backdoor of the wood frame house and acknowledged his mother's call. He waved back an OK to her and looked to Parks, "Let's get out of this cold."

Six months had passed since their final encounter with the outlaw sheriff, Jubal Thompson. Free and Parks had prevailed and were able to return all the money the Old Stone and Dodge ranches lost to the lawman's rustling operation. As a show of their gratitude, the ranchers offered them one thousand dollars each and persuaded Judge Freemont to reconsider his unfair court judgment against Free.

As they entered his mother's kitchen, the smells of coffee and fatback engulfed them filling Free's nostrils with childhood memories. He pulled a willow chair from the table and invited Parks to sit, then walked toward the iron wood stove, removed a blackened kettle, and poured two cups of coffee. He handed Parks one of the tin cups and sat across from him.

"Who wants eggs?" Martha asked.

Free pressed against the back of his chair and watched

his mother set a plate of eggs and fatback in front of him. "Oh that smells wonderful."

"And there are biscuits coming," Clara said.

Free glanced up and watched his bride of five months enter the kitchen. Clara had nourished and cared for him while he sat in Jubal Thompson's jail months earlier. And it was Clara who rode alone into the Comancheria to save both Parks and him from the hangman's noose. He could not imagine life without Clara. Beaming at her beauty, he noticed she carried a piece of leather with one hand while she finished a stitch with the other.

"All right, Free Anderson," Clara said, "this is for you."

Free accepted the object from Clara, a handcrafted tobacco pouch.

"It's about time," Parks laughed.

Free hung the pouch around his neck and then pointed to Parks, "Can I borrow some of your tobacco to put in here?" Free feigned ignorance as the kitchen erupted in laughter and accusation.

"Free Anderson! You will get your own tobacco!" Clara laughed.

Free pulled an end cut of plug tobacco from his front shirt pocket and held it for the others to observe. "I want everyone to know I bought some yesterday at Dutch Nance's store."

He pushed a fork full of eggs toward his mouth, and then smiled as those around him applauded his purchase. He looked toward Parks and said, "Well you can't say we have occasion for fuss in our lives these days."

The words had no sooner left his mouth when a thunder of buggy wheels rumbled throughout the kitchen. Free threw a surprised glance toward the door.

"What was that you said, Sergeant?" Parks asked.

Free hurried to the kitchen window and saw Murph Jenkins running stiffly toward the house. A rapid series of knocks echoed on the cut cedar, and Free rushed to open the door.

"What is it, Mr. Jenkins?" Free reached out and pulled the white-haired man into the warmth of the kitchen.

"You and Parks need to come quick!"

Parks rose, "Trouble?"

"It's Samuel! Those mustangs of yours he leased out earlier in the week came back this morning in bad shape. Samuel called the two cowboys on it and told them they would have to pay a week's worth of keep for how they treated those ponies."

Free sat Mr. Jenkins down in one of the willow chairs. "Mother, get him some coffee please." He held the hotel proprietor by the shoulders and asked. "What happened next?"

"They beat him and laughed while they did it. Samuel's gashed deep on his forehead, and he keeps spitting up blood."

"Where is he?" Parks asked.

"He's at the hotel, but the army doc is out at the Wittson Ranch helping Sarah Holder with her baby. Samuel needs some doctoring soon, or I am sure he's gonna die. Those cowboys were mean sorts, all liquored up and playing to the gallery."

Free glanced up and saw Clara was already preparing a bag. Before their marriage, she worked for Murph as a maid and nurse. "Clara will ride back with you, Mr. Jenkins." He patted the man's arm in reassurance.

"I knew you'd come. Thank you, Clara."

"And those cowboys, where are they?" Parks asked.

"The both of them are in Kelley's drinking."

The Flats lay eight miles to the south of Free's homestead. Following the Clear Fork, both men rode in silence in the cold until Fort Griffin came into view.

"What are you aiming to do, Parks?"

"I reckon if these boys are roostered enough to beat a helpless man like Samuel, not much good is fixing to come out of this."

"Likely so," Free said. He pulled his Colt from its holster and checked his ammo.

"It would be nice if the county could find a new sheriff," Parks said.

"You and I both know they aren't going to get anyone to take the job. They won't pay near enough for a man with any sense to risk his neck sheriffing The Flats." Free slid the Colt back in its cover.

"Especially when they know we're dumb enough to do it for nothing," Parks replied.

CHAPTER 2

The Flats, Texas December 1868

Parks tied Horse to the hitching post in front of Kelley's and then stepped onto the boardwalk with a heedful look in each direction. He needed to make sure he and Free entered the saloon without a surprise attack from behind them. To the west he saw Milt Davies approaching rapidly, waving his hand in the air.

"Parks!" The man hollered.

Parks stopped on the boardwalk and waited for the Kelley's regular to make his way to him and Free.

"Parks, thank goodness you two are here," Milt said. "Two hard cases are inside. They gave Samuel a beating this morning, and now they've run everyone out of the bar. They need dealing with before they kill someone."

"They the only two in the bar, Milt?" Parks kept his gaze on the saloon doors.

"Yep. One of them is tall and heavyset; he's the one who beat Samuel."

"OK. Thanks, Milt, you just go on about your business, Free and I will take care of this."

Parks watched Milt walk back to the hotel. A tingling warning traveled through his body and made the hairs on his arms stand at attention. He knew this fight or flight response manifested when danger was imminent, signaling that he and Free might be walking into an ambush. He rubbed his gun handle for security and then glanced to Free. "I'm going in first and see where these boys are situated. You give me a minute and then come in and set yourself on the opposite side of the bar from them."

"Be careful, Parks."

Inside the bar, Parks noticed the two cowboys standing off to the left in front of the Faro and Chuck-a-Luck tables. Both had a good view of the swinging doors and anyone who tried to enter the saloon. He walked to the middle of the bar and surveyed the room. Mr. Kelley ran a dirty rag in and out of a glass, nodded at his approach, and then slightly tilted his head toward the cowboys.

"What'll it be, Parks?"

"Tobacco." Parks placed both his hands on the bar.

Parks watched as Kelley set a wooden bowl filled with tobacco on the counter. He cut a plug off one of the ends and nodded back to the owner.

"The bar's closed right now, cowboy."

Parks swung a hard gaze over to the pair. He looked at the taller of the two, the one doing the talking. "You must be the cowboy who spent all week breaking down my ponies." Parks spit brown liquid toward the cuspidor at his feet.

"Oh, those were your nags; well, I guess we beat the wrong man then." The heavyset cowboy laughed.

The hinges of the saloon door creaked. Parks glanced up at the bar mirror and saw Free enter. He turned his gaze to the cowboys and noticed the talker tossing back a shot of whiskey.

"Ain't this nice, they let coloreds drink with white folks in this burg."

Free moved to the east end of the bar and leaned on the wooden counter. He stared across at the cowboys.

"Morning, Free."

"Morning, Mr. Kelley."

Parks spit once more, and then glanced toward the end of

the bar. He stood, back held straight, hands clenched in tight fists, and proceeded point-blank for the talker.

"You might want to watch yourself, horse peddler. I don't take kindly to a man getting too close to me." The cowboy moved his right hand below the bar in a slow deliberate motion.

Keeping his eyes locked on the cowboy, Parks rounded the corner of the bar with hard purpose, coming face to face with the man. He saw the cowboy's hand wrapped around an ivory pistol handle.

"You've got some nerve," the man uttered.

In one quick motion, Parks' left hand surrounded the cowboy's pistol grip, and using his strength, he held the man's Colt in its holster.

"Arrrg." The cowboy groaned as his knuckles cracked against metal.

With lightning speed, Parks pulled his own Colt and thrust the barrel against the cowboy's cheekbone while releasing his grip from the man's pistol. "Go ahead and pull that Colt, cowboy! Let's see how you back up your wind!"

"And you!" Free barked across the bar to the man's companion. "Set your hands on the bar!"

Parks made sure the cowboy's companion moved his hands onto the bar as ordered, then looked back to the talker. Forcing his Colt deeper into the cowboy's cheek, he said, "Now big talker, I believe you owe Samuel twenty-five dollars for his injuries, and you owe me another eight dollars for the horses."

"You're gonna regret this, horseman. You better kill me now because I'll come back looking for you after we're done here today!"

A surge of energy gushed through Park's chest. Without a second thought, he raised his left hand and whacked the cowboy hard across the mouth. He watched the man dip and then wipe his mouth with the back of his hand; a trickle of blood was visible on the corner of his mouth. "You're not dealing with an old livery owner now, Cowboy!" Darkness clouded the cowboy's eyes. Parks figured this affair could end only one way. "Now, you reach deep into your pocket, cowboy, and pull out some dollars. If you don't have any, you and your friend are gonna spend considerable time in the jail! Understand?"

With angry reluctance, the cowboy thrust a hand into his pocket and pulled out a roll of cash, his face flushed scarlet as he slapped his money onto the bar.

Parks looked to Kelley and said, "Count out thirty-three dollars from his roll and hang onto it for me."

Kelley moved toward them, counted out the money, and then placed the cowboy's roll back on the bar.

"Now Cowboy, pick up the rest of your money and you and your friend get out of here! And from now on, you best ride clear of The Flats! The next time I see you I won't be as friendly!"

Parks removed his gun from the man's cheek. He made sure he remained in full view of them as the pair ambled slowly out of the bar, his Colt pointed steady at the swinging doors. Particles of dust drifted slowly into the saloon, highlighted by the morning sun and propelled by the door's movements, they flickered briefly before settling on the planked floor. He motioned with his Colt for Free to get down. And then moving right, he braced his shoulder against the inside wall of the saloon.

The doors leveled, and the brief silence was violated as the talker burst back inside, his gun drawn. He sprayed lead toward the west corner of the bar, filling the room with smoke.

"I knew you were too stupid to leave with breath in your lungs, Cowboy!" Parks' Colt roared. He catapulted the cowboy back through the swinging doors with a single shot.

Parks looked over to Free as he rose from behind the bar.

"Hey, you," Parks yelled out to the second cowboy. "When I walk out these doors if I see a pistol in your hands, I will shoot you as dead as your friend!"

Parks held for an instant and then heard the jingle of spurs on the boardwalk hightailing it away. He pushed through the swinging doors, stepped over the cowboy lying on his back in the street and glanced west. He saw the cowboy's companion hurrying toward Fort Griffin.

"This one's dead," Free said.

"You know this fella, Kelley?" Parks asked. "Samuel told me he leased him horses to ride to Fort Concho, but he didn't give me any names."

"I know of him," Kelley answered. "Parks, that's Tig Hardy's younger brother, Chase."

"Who's Tig Hardy?" Free asked.

Kelley kicked at the body with his boot. "He's the man who bushwhacked those three Buffalo Soldiers of the 10th Cavalry outside of Fort Concho. Story goes he killed all three and then cut off their chevrons. He's a detestable character who's locked up in the jail at the fort awaiting trial."

"You think this cowboy and his friend rode our mustangs the eighty miles to Fort Concho?" Free asked.

Parks looked toward the stage depot and tightened his jaw. "Would appear so, and my gut's telling me Tig Hardy is no longer in jail. What do you think Tig's gonna do when he learns his brother is dead?"

Kelley sized up the younger Hardy's body. "I suspect he's gonna come looking for the man who done his brother in."

"I reckon that's so." Parks stared grimly at the corpse. "Free, why don't you check on Samuel while I get this body moved off the street."

In an upstairs room of the Jenkins House, Free stood next to Clara and looked down on the sleeping figure of the livery owner. "How's he doing?"

"Not good, Free. I got his head wound sewed up, but blood keeps oozing from his mouth. I'm afraid he's busted up inside, and I don't know of anything to stop that."

At that moment, Free saw Samuel roll his eyes open.

"Free, I'm sorry about those horses."

Free knelt beside the bed and noticed the blood dripping from the corner of the livery owner's mouth. "Don't worry about that right now, Samuel. I need to ask you a couple of questions."

"Sure," Samuel whispered.

"Did either of those cowboys tell you where they wanted to take the mustangs?"

"They said Fort Concho. The big man said they were prospecting for land."

"But those ponies could easily make the San Angelo trip," Free stated. He scratched his head in confusion.

"That's just it, Free; those ponies had been rode hard, more than to San Angelo and back. I swear they had to be run over a thousand miles."

Free patted Samuel's arm and stood. "You just rest, Samuel. Clara will stay here with you until you're better." He watched the man nod his head and then slowly close his eyes. Turning to Clara, he rubbed her shoulder, and then he drew her close. "Thanks for helping here."

"What's troubling you, Free?"

He smiled at her ability to read his moods. "Something isn't right here, Clara, but danged if I know what."

CHAPTER 3

Paracoa Spring, Guadalupe Mountains, Texas
December 1868

Tig Hardy poked at a burning log with the heel of his boot. Seven hundred feet into the Guadalupes, the cool morning air and the wait caused a troubling anxiety to build in his head. The mountain's silence, gladly received, found interruption only by the occasional crack of a pine splinter incinerated in the fire.

Chase and his friend Jordie should have returned by now, Tig reckoned. Something didn't feel right, but if he knew his younger brother, he was bedded down with a bottle of Lone Jack sleeping off a bender. Ignoring his instincts to move on, he decided to wait one more day for the pair. If they hadn't showed by then, he would meet up with the rest of the gang at the old Pinery Station, now long abandoned by the Butterfield Coach line.

The escape from the Fort Concho stockade had gone exactly as he planned. Lady fortune smiled on him the day the mustang pony arrived at the fort. Although he remained in the stockade during the races, later his guards willingly described the contest for him. One pony, small as a donkey, had run five times without rest against the cavalry's best and beaten them all. The mustang's owner, the guards recounted, told all in attendance that his horses could run a hundred miles a day for a week on a handful of grain. As the soldiers recited the race repeatedly during the remainder of the day, Tig absorbed it all and contrived his break away.

And he had proof that those mustang ponies had performed as talked up, for he now sat five hundred miles northwest of Fort Concho unloose from a sure hanging. And if Chase did as he was told, the mustangs were more than a hundred miles northeast of Fort Concho. Tig laughed aloud. "My trail should be colder than those 10th Cavalry soldiers by now," he mused.

A loud series of caws stirred Tig from his thoughts and caused him to swing his head to the south. Three crows took flight from the pines. The departing birds' momentum forced the tree branches against each other, further breaking the silence of the mountain. Turning an ear toward the crows, Tig slid the Colt from his holster and held the gun beneath the saddle blanket that covered his torso. A lone rider exited a break of pine fifty yards away and galloped toward the camp.

As the man drew close, he could see it was Jordie. Even at the distance, Jordie's face carried a look of dread. Tig stood as Jordie heeled the horse several feet from the fire. He walked over, grabbed the horse's reins, and stared at his brother's friend with spiteful scorn.

"Tig! Man, am I glad I found you!" Jordie shouted.

"Where's Chase, Jordie?" Tig looked down the trail behind him.

"We ran into trouble in The Flats."

"Where's Chase?"

"He beat the livery owner, Tig—."

"I said where's Chase, Jordie!"

"He's dead, Tig. Shot down in the saloon there."

"What?" Tig squeezed hard on the reins, wrapping them in a knot around his hand. "Chase is dead?" He looked up at Jordie in disbelief. "Who shot him?"

"It was an ambush, Tig. Two cowboys in town, one white and one colored, bushwhacked him as he walked in the saloon."

Tig stared at the ground, trying to comprehend his brother's death. "Bushwhacked?"

"One was hid behind the door. Shot him dead as he walked into the saloon."

Tig threw his head up. "Chase just walked into the bar, and these cowboys shot him up?"

"As sure as I'm breathing, Tig. That's what happened."

Tig exhaled loudly. Something didn't sound right. "How'd you get out?"

"I ain't gonna lie to you, Tig. Once that cowboy shot Chase, I ran. I ran for my life."

Tig stared at the man in front of him. "So you just took a French leave?" He thought hard about shooting Jordie off his horse but reckoned he would need him to identify his brother's murderer. Dropping the horse's reins, he cursed in a low breath and then yelled, "Git down off your horse, Jordie, and explain everything that came about. And I mean everything!"

Minutes later, both men sat at the fire. Tig stared hard into the flame muttering, "If you two had just done what I said, we would all be in Fort Sumner right now in fine shape. But Chase always had to go crazy, and now he's dead for the cause of it."

"He just went crazy like you said, Tig."

"Shut-up, Jordie! I ought to kill you for not helping him or killing the man who shot him."

"But I told you, Tig, I didn't know he was going back in the saloon. There was nothing I could do."

"Well, there's something you're gonna do now, Jordie."

"Anything, you know that, Tig."

Tig took a deep breath and recalled his father's strict instructions on family. *The only way a Hardy man mourns a kinfolk's killing is with revenge, Tig. It was that way with my daddy and his daddy before him. It's always been our way.*

A darkness clouded Tig's eyes. "We're both going back. You're gonna point out that cowboy, and then you and me are going to kill him and his colored friend. Then we're going to kill everyone in both their families." He stared at the scared man across from him. "That's what we're gonna do, Jordie."

CHAPTER 4

Fort Concho, Texas December 1868

The cold front which now pushed to the east, left behind the accustomed temperate days of December. Riding to where the North and Middle Concho rivers converged, Free gazed at the stone structures of Fort Concho. The fort sat on what looked to Free to be an endless flatness.

"Is there any vegetation without thorns that grows in this country?" Free pulled mescat barbs from the sleeve of his shirt.

"You're supposed to ride around 'em, Sergeant. Not through them." Parks grinned at his friend's annoyance.

"That's a heap easier said than done." Free shucked the last thorn and watched as small drops of red bubbled upward dotting his sweat-stained shirt.

The men stepped down from their mounts and wrapped their reins around the hitching post near the quartermaster building. They had come to Fort Concho seeking answers to the mystery of the Hardy brothers, and most important, if Tig Hardy still sat in lock-up.

"Parks, Free, to what do I owe the honor?" Captain Huntt walked the men into his quarters.

The men strode into the foyer behind him removing their hats as they entered.

"I will tell you both, my men do so treasure those mustangs you sold us. My goodness, they are magnificent beasts! And I can speak with authority that many of my colleagues are now interested in buying horses from you."

"Thank you, sir." Parks smiled at the captain and cleared his throat. "And please excuse my rudeness, Captain, but we were wondering if you could give us some information on a recent guest of yours."

The captain motioned for Parks and Free to sit. "Who would that guest be?"

"Tig Hardy," Parks answered.

"Ah. Tig Hardy. It seems Mr. Hardy is no longer our guest. I can only surmise he found the accommodations not to his liking and decided to find a setting more suited to his person."

"Any idea where he might be?" Free asked.

Captain Huntt reached over to his desk and removed a plug of tobacco. "Appears the man just up and disappeared." He held the plug toward Parks and Free. "We searched a hundred miles in every direction for him and never found a trace."

Free reached out and took the tobacco from the captain. "How'd he get out?"

"Well for that, I will give him his due. There was a man who looked just like him, drinking across the river at Mestizo's—."

Parks leaned forward with a furrowed brow. "Just like him?"

The captain leaned back against his chair and ran a hand across his forehead. "Could have been kin," he said almost to himself. He then sat up straight and took a deep breath. "Embarrassing as it is to recount, someone on post, probably another accomplice, began shouting, *Tig Hardy's leaving out of Mestizo's!* Soon most of the fort was saddling up and chasing the fake Tig as he rode south to beat the devil."

"What happened when your troops caught up with him?" Free asked.

"There was not a lot we could do, Free. It obviously was not Tig. Up close we could tell the man looked like him, but that was all."

"Meanwhile, the real Tig flew the coop?" Parks asked.

"That's the long and short of it, Parks. The boys knew what they were doing. They executed their plan while most of the troops were out in the field. One detachment was escorting civilian stonemasons and workers from Fredericksburg as protectors from that crazy Comanche Little Bear and his band. The second detachment was searching for White Horse. Since Custer's victory on the Washita, White Horse is back in Texas on the warpath and stealing livestock at will. To further complicate the situation, almost everyone on the post was at the mess hall taking their noon meal."

"Any idea of the other accomplice's identity?" Free handed the tobacco back to the captain.

"None. We figured he busted the lock while the rest of the post went chasing the imposter."

"What about the imposter, captain?" Parks asked. "Who was he?"

"That's another mistake made by my men. Once they saw the man wasn't Tig, they apologized and quick-timed it back to the fort, leaving the imposter to skedaddle. And by this time, the pursuing troops were ten miles to the south of the fort and probably in the opposite direction of the real Tig." The captain leaned forward and stared at both men with hard eyes. "Now, you two want to tell me why you're asking all these questions?"

Parks raised his head and bit down on his lip. "Yes, sir. I shot your fake Tig in The Flats yesterday."

"What?" the captain asked.

"The owner of Kelley's, down in The Flats, identified the man as Chase Hardy, Tig's little brother."

"I still don't understand." The captain frowned.

"Well, sit back, Captain," Free lifted his hat slightly and

scratched his head. "Because this story is going to interest you."

After Free finished his tale, Captain Huntt stood and walked to the small frame window in his study. Looking out over the parade grounds, he spoke, "You are aware, I would assume, of the reason behind Tig's stay in our stockade?"

Free stood and walked over toward the captain. "Talk is he killed three Buffalo Soldiers from the 10th Cavalry across the river."

Captain Huntt turned and faced Free. "He didn't just kill them, Free. He mutilated the three. Cut off their chevrons, ripped the stripes from their pants, and then disfigured the corpses. And the strangest part, those soldiers weren't even from around here. Tig didn't even know the men. They came out of Fort Sill to help with the telegraph lines near Johnson's Station. The way I hear it, they were done with their job and decided to bend an elbow before heading back through Indian Territory."

Parks stood, a dark frown furrowed his brow. "What was his difficulty?"

"Miguel Telodes, the Mexican who runs Mestizo's, came running across the Concho screaming like a gut-shot panther. He said Tig went crazy because the colored soldiers were drinking and dancing with a couple of Mexican girls."

Free shook his head in disgust. "What possesses a man to feel so obliged as to another man's drinking companion?"

"I wish I could speak to that, Free. All I can tell you is Tig was sitting at a table drinking Lone Jack when we arrived. He didn't resist or even act like three soldiers were lying dead around the bar. He was as calm as you or me right now. Most uncomfortable thing I've ever seen."

Free looked to Parks and saw the concern gathering about his face. "I reckon Mr. Hardy will be looking to pay us a visit soon."

"You best be extra careful." The captain walked the men toward the study door and shook hands with each one. "Tig Hardy won't rest until you've paid with family the same as him."

Free and Parks hurried without distraction from Huntt's quarters to their ponies. The distance between themselves and family occupied each man's concentration and presented a harsh reality. The prospect of the long ride home anguished both of them.

Free mounted Spirit and looked toward Parks. "You best get to San Saba, Parks, I'm riding for the Clear Fork."

"I'll move my mother in with friends, Free; then I'll come straight away." Parks wheeled Horse toward the Concho River.

"Ride safe," Free yelled. He slapped the reins across Spirit's shoulders and spurred the mustang hard for the scrub prairie and northeast toward home.

CHAPTER 5

Anderson Homestead, Texas December 1868

Clara trudged in the soft river sand and hauled a bucket of water toward the mustang pens. She spent most of her day in The Flats tending to Samuel. She returned home only after the army doctor finally made his way to the Jenkins House hotel.

Shadows crept sluggishly across the prairie and unfurled a tenuous canvas of black in their retreat. Feeling the warmth of the December day disappearing, Clara hurried to finish her outdoor chores. As she crossed the limestone porch at the back of the house, her attention was drawn toward the distinctive bark of a dog. Shading her eyes, she scanned the open prairie toward a spot where a mound of beads, rock bowls and hair pipes lay. In the midst of these Kiowa offerings, she saw an Indian dog tied to a decorated lance by a length of rawhide. The animal jumped excitedly on its hind legs, pulling against its binding and barking at the empty prairie.

"Another gift?" Martha Anderson asked from the back porch.

"It appears that way, Mother." Clara moved with prudent apprehension toward the dog. It resembled a large coyote. "Parks says as long as the Kiowa believe Free is responsible for the recent rains, they will continue to leave gifts in hopes the buffalo will return."

"Well, we best leave him tied for now," Martha held a fixed

stare on the confused animal. “It doesn’t look to me much like he wants to stay here. I’ll fetch him some table scraps in a bit.”

Clara nodded and gazed out over the prairie. She was concerned that the Kiowa could unexpectedly appear without their presence being known. “Maybe, he’ll be a good thing, Mother. You know, to warn us and all.”

“I don’t know, Clara, if I have to listen to something yapping all night, I’d much rather it be a baby.” Martha looked at her daughter-in-law and pursed her lips together. “When is that going to happen? I’m getting on in years, you know.”

“Why, Mother Anderson!” Clara leaned her head back and pushed her tongue slightly through her lips, “You never know; it might be happening now.”

Martha looked carefully at Clara, letting her daughter-in-law’s words slowly sink in. “Clara!” She beamed broadly, “Are you—? You tell me now! Am I going to be a grandmother?”

Clara nodded her head and held her arms out. The two women embraced and jumped up and down in each other’s arms, their shouts carried across the Comancheria.

“Two months, I believe.” Clara tasted the salt of tears in her mouth.

“Clara!” Martha held her daughter-in-law at arm’s length, “Does Free know?”

Clara shook her head, “Not yet. I wanted to be sure before telling him.”

Martha embraced Clara once more and rubbed her stomach. “A baby! We’re going to have baby!”

Well into the night Clara was bolted awake by an unfamiliar noise. The Indian dog’s unremitting barking was now silent, and a strange stillness reigned over the house and surrounding prairie. The fog of sleep still present, she rubbed her eyes and tried to recall the sound that brought her upright.

Still drowsy, she let her feet dangle off the side of the bed. Out of the corner of her eye she saw a flicker through the open bedroom window. Suddenly, the black night glowed orange.

"Oh no! No!" She watched the flames soar skyward, burning through the newly constructed corral, "Mother Anderson! Fire! The corral's on fire!" She sprang from the bed, threw on her work clothes and hurried to the kitchen door.

Outside, the heat of the blaze kept her well away from the now fully engulfed structure. From behind, she felt arms surround her. Weeping, she cried, "The horses, Mother! What about the horses?"

"Make no mistake, Miss. I ain't your mother."

Clara felt the hands tighten on her shoulder. Using all her strength, she turned and stared into the face of a huge man, his fire-lit face was that of the devil. "Who are you?" she stammered.

Grasping her with one hand, the man removed his hat, "The name's Tig Hardy."

Clara watched the man replace his hat and then looked on helplessly as a massive fist came her way.

Clara felt a sticky wetness on her lips. She tried to move her tongue, but it seemed stuck on the inside of her cheek. A rough grit scratched her jaw, and for some reason, the world seemed sideways. Focusing toward the illuminated prairie, she could see the Indian dog facing her. *Strange*, she thought, *it's as if the lance is sticking out of his side*. She pushed her chin down against her chest and saw the last of the flames burning out in the corral. *Thank God, the fire's out*. Then she was lifted up.

"You might want to watch this, Ma'm."

In shock, Clara turned toward another face, "Who are you?" she asked.

"Name's Jordie." The man removed an unused safety match

from his mouth. "Here's something to remember me by." He poked the match into her shirt pocket.

"But what are you—."

"Shhh. Now just watch, there." The man shook her toward the corner of the house.

Clara tried to focus on the spot. Blinking her eyes to clear her vision, she saw Martha lying on her back, the bigger man straddling her.

"Now, Miss," the big man spoke to her, "where is your man?"

"What?" Clara tried to make sense of the goings on.

"Wrong answer."

Clara watched as the man brought his huge fist down on Martha's face.

"Noooo!" Clara screamed, struggling against the man holding her, "Leave her be! Leave her be!"

"I'll ask again. Where's your man?"

"Don't you tell this man anything!" Martha shrieked.

"Why are you doing this?" Clara screamed.

"Wrong again." The man delivered another heavy blow to Martha's cheekbone. A wide circle of red welted up on her face, visible even in the night's darkness; a river of blood flowed from her left nostril. "We can do this all night, Miss, but to tell you the truth, I don't think the old lady is gonna hold on for very long."

Clara struggled, trying to tear free from her captor. "Hold on! I'll tell you! I'll tell you! Just don't hurt her anymore!" The thought of giving away Free's location pained her heart, but she knew Martha could not suffer through another battering from the hulk atop her.

"Now that's better." The big man grinned. His countenance showed a terrifying evil. "Where is he?"

"He's at Fort Concho." Clara felt her shoulders dip as she cried from both anguish and pain. The big man stood, leaving Martha writhing on the ground.

“That’s too bad,” he said and walked toward Clara, “He’s a far piece from here.” Tig stopped in front of her and took a moment to think. “I’ll take her Jordie,” he grabbed for Clara, “You burn the house to the ground.”

The three-room house caught quickly. Tied to a horse, Clara could only stare down at Martha. *Was she dreaming?* From out of the veil of fog and tears she heard the big man speak to Martha and knew this was no nightmare.

“Ma’m, you need to hang in there and don’t die too soon. I need you to give the colored and his cowboy friend a message. I need you to tell them Tig Hardy has his woman, and I’ll meet them out west in the Guadalupes. You hear? I need for you to be sure and tell them that.”

Suddenly, Clara felt her body jerk backwards as a loud whoop from Tig Hardy set her horse running. Then the blackness of the Comancheria surrounded her.

CHAPTER 6

Clear Fork Country, Texas December 1868

Although he knew the better, Free kept Spirit on the move all night. Running a horse across a moonless prairie was a foolish and downright dangerous folly. But he knew he would not have been able to sleep anyway, so he left camp and plied his time walking and leading Spirit over the darkened landscape. A persistent dread unnerved him. The image of Tig Hardy harming his family had clamped onto his thoughts like a Clear Fork snapping turtle.

As the first sign of light pushed through a generous sky of clouds, he mounted and took Spirit on a hard run along the upper bank of the Clear Fork. The slender native grasses separated with a whoosh as he rode by, spraying seed head along the ground. Usually alert to his surroundings, he kept a singular focus on home, not sure of what landmarks he passed along the way.

By noon, he saw the rising smoke from the bakery at Fort Griffin and knew he was only miles away from Clara. "Com'on Spirit," he pleaded, and once more he implored the reins to hasten the mustang toward home.

Around the last bend of the Clear Fork, just before his stake, he pulled hard on Spirit's reins and drew back in the saddle. He stared ahead in total disbelief at the smoldering remains of his house and corral. His home lay reduced to piles of charred rubble. The dull, overpowering smell of charcoal hung in the air and plowed its way through his nostrils. "My God!" he shouted, and then, "Clara!"

He frantically took spurs to Spirit and galloped across the plain. "Clara! Mother!" he screamed at the sky.

He rode through the farmyard in a spray of dust. Where the kitchen once stood, he saw a shape lying lifeless on the ground. "No! No! No!" he cried and jumped from the saddle before Spirit could stop. The sudden leap propelled him forward, causing him to stumble and fall several feet in front of the form that was his mother. "Mother!" His anguish and anger penetrated and hung in the dust filled air. "Who did this?" He knelt over his mother and looked at her mangled features. A huge swelling engulfed the entire left side of her face and caused her left eye to close. Her nose lay flattened against her right cheek, and an eerie rattle accompanied every breath. With great care, he lifted her head and held her in silence, his eyes closed in fear.

"Free?"

Free opened his eyes and looked down at his mother's face. "Mother! It's going to be OK." His lips mouthed thank you God as tears filled his eyes, "It's going to be OK, now."

"Free."

"Shhhhshh." He whispered. "Don't talk. It's OK."

"They took Clara."

Free looked all around the property and realized Clara was nowhere to be seen. "Who, Mother?" he pleaded, "Who took her?"

"He said to tell you he was going to the Guadalupes."

Free knew the answer, but he felt compelled to hear the name vocalized, "Who, Mother? Who was it?"

"He called himself Tig Hardy."

Free constructed a lean-to shelter from a piece of charred roof and placed his mother underneath, laying her on Spirit's saddle blanket. The wood reeked of smoke, but the structure offered protection from the afternoon sun. Using his bandana and water from his canteen, he gently cleaned her bloody face and then lowered her head back onto his bedroll. He stared at her once smooth features now disfigured by the bruises and swelling.

Staring west, he faced a dilemma that tore at his soul. Clara was kidnapped and taken to the far reaches of West Texas. His mother, badly hurt, could not survive the afternoon without a doctor's help. Fear encased his heart. He was afraid to leave his mother's side, and he was afraid to stay. This inner turmoil caused his belly to ache and his head to pound. Left with no good choices, he remained, wiping her head with his damp bandana and talking quiet-like to her.

Later, with his mother sleeping, the disposition of the day turned to silence. The only lull in the strange calm was the quiet whisper of a soft wind blowing from the north. Carried within the air current came the low whimper of what sounded like a dog. Free raised his head and held his ear to the sound. The weak cry was pitiful and unnerving. He looked into the north wind and held sight of the Kiowa offerings several yards into the prairie. There in the grass he saw the Kiowa lance waving in the wind.

He hurried out to the sacred spot and saw the dog. The animal was pinned to the ground by the lance. Free stroked the animal's head and spoke in a comforting voice. "Easy there, fella. I'm just going to see if we can get this spear out of you." He felt the dog's side and saw that the lance had pushed through the animal's hide from the rib cage to the backbone, but it had not penetrated beyond the flesh. Reaching under the dog's back, he held the lance above its imbedded point and snapped the wooden shaft. With the lance tip removed, he pulled the shaft from the dog's side. "How's that?" he asked.

The dog turned his head toward the wounds and began licking the punctures with long sweeps of his tongue.

Free issued a low whistle causing Spirit to perk up his ears. "Com'on Spirit," he called. "We need some water over here." The mustang nodded his head and snorted, and then moved toward Free.

Free removed his canteen and knelt beside the dog. He poured water into an open palm held at the dog's mouth. The animal lapped at the water with a wolfish thirst. When the dog had his fill, he continued to lick Free's hand. Free stood and turned back to Spirit. He removed a small piece of dried beef from his saddle-pack and offered it to the dog.

The dog smelled the meat and tried to rise but could achieve only a half-sitting position. "You rest," Free said as he fed the beef to the dog. "You can get up later."

Seeing he had done all he could for the animal, he moved back to his sleeping mother's side and sat beside her. Once seated, a rush of images of Clara overwhelmed his mind and created a melancholy that tore at his soul.

Later, the anger came. Anger at his helplessness. Anger at his mother's condition. Anger at Clara's kidnapping and, most of all, anger that he now owed Tig Hardy a debt of blood and revenge.

"Free?"

At the sound of his name, Free's eyes popped open. He turned to his mother. He noticed her eyes gazed upward on the lean-to.

"Free, where's the sky?" she asked.

Free struggled to rise, aware he had finally given in to his need for sleep. Gaining his balance, he tried to make sense of her question. "What is it, Mother?"

"Free, I want to see the sky."

He gently brushed the top of her head and took a measure

of her eyes. Both pupils appeared light and glazed. "Sure, Mother." He pushed the lean-to away, exposing an endless blue. "There you go. It's a beautiful sky today."

"Free? Where is it? I can't seem to find it."

Free felt a wave of tears engulf his vision. He lifted her head and held her tight against his chest. "It's right there, Mother." He gazed skyward, "It's all blue today. It's as fine a day as we've had in awhile."

"Free."

He leaned in close, trying to comprehend her nearly inaudible words, "Yes, Mother?" He watched as one faint tear balled up in the corner of her swollen eye. Garnering all his strength, he tried hard to keep from choking on his emotion.

"Free, Clara's with child."

"What. . .?" He pulled her tight into his chest.

"Clara's going to have a baby?"

"A baby, Free. . . A grandbaby." Martha stared blankly at the sky and released a small gasp of breath.

Free lifted his mother against his chest and slowly rocked her back and forth. It was the same way she would rock him as a child when he was frightened or worried. He remembered her touch, strong but soft, and he recalled her soothing voice when she would sing the slave lullaby, "I Live in the Other World."

He began to hum the song to his mother in a crackled whisper. After a short time, he looked down on her face, the lines of time though etched deeply, provided her with striking beauty. Through his tears he saw a peaceful gaze settled over her. He looked away, unable to watch her eyes roll upward toward the heavens.

"No!" He cried aloud. "Mother! You can't leave me now! Not now!"

Below the charred ruins of his house and near the river, Free laid his Mother to rest among a stand of pecan and black walnut trees. He wrapped her in his bedroll and mounded the grave with river rock to keep her safe.

He recited the Twenty-Third Psalm, then walked back to the burned out house and carved a message onto the charred lean-to with his knife.

Parks

Mother is killed and Clara is taken to the Guadalupes

I am riding there to find her

Free

December 20 .

CHAPTER 7

Agua de Mesteño, Texas December 1868

After riding all night and most of the morning, Tig surveyed a junction of small tributaries belonging to the Colorado. The broken land, interspersed with thickets of scrub and prickly pear, held a stream of water forty feet across and not much deeper than a man's ankle. The Spanish called this place *Agua de Mesteño*. Below him, the trading tent of Nathan Polk remained open for business even though the season grew late. Tig knew this was the last chance for whiskey and jerked beef before completing the crossing into New Mexico and then down to the now deserted old Pinery Way Station.

He glanced back at Jordie and the woman who were stopped several yards behind. It would be foolish to ride into Polk's with the woman. Holding a female captive, no matter her color, didn't sit well with most men who rode the trail, and he sure didn't need that reputation following him through West Texas. His dilemma was he couldn't trust Jordie to ride into Polk's, and he couldn't trust him to stay with the woman. *I probably should have shot him the day he rode into the Guadalupes,* he thought.

"Jordie!" he called out.

"Yeah, Tig!"

"I'm going to ride down to Polk's. You stay here with the woman and set up a camp. You tie her up and watch her close. I should be back before dark."

"I'll watch her, Tig. Just like you say," Jordie called out.

"And, Jordie, you keep awake until I get back!"

The trading tent of Nathan Polk was no more than a lean-to covered in deer hide. In front of the structure, Nathan Polk relaxed on a large, square rock and whittled on a piece of river wood.

Tig rode into the camp and looked about with a caution.

"Welcome, Tig," Nathan said without looking up, "word up the trail has you behind bars in the Fort Concho stockade."

Tig looked at the trader, and snarled, "Appears not, Polk. Appears I'm here."

"So you be." Nathan smiled. "What can I do you for?"

"I'm in need of some goods, but first I need a pull of Lone Jack."

"I think I can help," The trader pointed to another rock close by. "Tie up your horse, and sit a'spell."

Clara, free of the saddle, but still bound at the wrists, sat on the cold, rocky ground. Jordie knelt at her feet tying her ankles together.

"This oughta keep you from running," he smiled, and patted her secured feet.

Clara looked around her surroundings. She was exhausted from the ride through the night and most of the day, but with Tig gone, she knew this might be her only opportunity for escape. "You know he's going to kill you, Jordie," she stated matter of factly.

Jordie, now gathering twigs and scrub to start a fire, stopped and looked over. "You don't know what you're saying, Tig needs my help."

"Think about it, Jordie, as soon as you point out my husband and Parks, Tig's going to kill you too."

Jordie looked back to his fire kindling, "I ain't listening to you no more; you're just trying to scare me."

"You should be scared, Jordie. You know Tig. Do you really think he's going to let the cowboy who ran while his brother died just walk away? I hope you're smarter than that, Jordie."

Jordie stopped and gazed in the direction of the trading tent. He pursed his lips and wrinkled his forehead.

"Your only chance is to run, Jordie. You better run now while Tig's down at the traders."

Jordie looked over to Clara. "He'd hunt me down."

"He's going to do that anyway. You need to run while you have time to put some distance between you and him."

Jordie glanced once more to the trader's tent. "And what about you?" he asked.

"You best carry me with you, Jordie," Clara spoke in a firm voice. "Otherwise, I'll tell Tig of your plan."

After several shots of whiskey, Tig looked at the trader's lot. In front of him on the riverbank lay two buffalo hides filled with a mixed bag of goods. To his right, the hide held an assortment of wampum, whiskey and brightly colored cloth for the Indian trade. Tig looked to his left and saw the whiskey, jerked meat and other dry goods for the whites.

"I'll be needing two days worth of beef, a bag of flour and a bottle of your whiskey, Nathan."

"I can furnish you with that." The grizzled trader stood, stretched his back and moved toward the buffalo hide. "You heading far?"

"I always thought you were a man smart enough to mind his own affairs." Tig threw a hard stare at the trader.

"No harm intended, Tig," Nathan tied a rawhide string around the bundle of dried beef. "Just wondering if you heard the news that Custer massacred a village of Cheyenne on the Washita. Killed old Black Kettle himself. The savages are on the warpath down here because of it. A man traveling alone needs to be extra careful."

Tig took the meat and stuffed the bundle into his saddle pack. "How much do I owe you, Nathan?"

The trader held out the whiskey and flour, "Ten bits ought to do it."

Tig stared down at the trader and then reached for the flour, "Might high, aren't we, Nathan?"

"It's the season's end, Tig." The trader shrugged his shoulders and then he looked toward the north, "The cold fronts will be moving in regular-like from here 'til spring."

Tig reached into his shirt and pulled out a few coins, "I thank you, Nathan." He flipped the coins toward the trader and then reached for the whiskey, "I'll carry this with me."

"Good luck to you, Tig."

Tig pulled himself up in the saddle and then looked down at the trader, "I trust you understand what I said about minding your own affairs."

Nathan looked up at Tig, "I think I understand plenty."

As the evening began its descent upon the land, Tig felt the chill of the late December air settle down his back. He spurred his horse up the modest hill that overlooked the trading post and anticipated the warmth of a scrub fire.

He cleared the incline up the hill and looked toward the place where he had left Jordie and the girl. "Jordie," he mumbled in anger. The small stand of scrub was dark. He couldn't smell smoke from the scrub or see the flicker of a fire. "Jordie!" He screamed out, "You better be working on a fire!"

Tig slapped the reins across the horse's shoulders and galloped for the scrub. In the small stand of oak, he dismounted and surveyed the area. There was no sign of fire makings or of Jordie and the woman. But in the settling darkness, he could just make out two sets of prints heading back south.

Realizing what had happened, he threw his head toward the purple sky, "I'll be coming for you, Jordie! I'll be coming!" His voice filled the dark expanse.

CHAPTER 8

Clear Fork Country, Texas December 1868

Parks laid spurs to Horse's flank and urged the mustang to a full gallop. Exhorting the animal down the main thoroughfare of The Flats, Parks pulled the reins sharply in front of the Jenkins House. With the abrupt stop, a swirl of dust swept over the pair and settled on the recently whitewashed porch.

Parks bounded out of the saddle and flipped Horse's reins over the cedar hitching post. With a jump, he hurried up the steps to the hotel where he confronted Milt Jenkins in the doorway. Milt's face creased with a look of trouble.

"What is it, Milt?"

"Parks, thank goodness you're back." Milt kept his head down and gazed intently at the boardwalk.

Parks reached out and grabbed the hotel proprietor by the shoulders, "What's going on, Milt?"

"It's Free," Milt began, "Josh Simpson's boy was out hunting rabbit near the Old Comanche Reservation this morning . . ."

"Get to it, Milt. Tell me what's happened?" Parks shook the man's shoulders, "Tell me!"

"The boy came back in a fuss, Parks. He said Free's place was burnt to the ground, and no one was to be seen around the place."

Parks released his grip, stepped back and leaned against an oak column under the hotel entrance overhang. "The boy didn't see anyone?"

"A group of us was preparing to head out there, Parks, just as you rode up."

"Where's the boy, Milt? I need to speak with him."

"Won't do you much good. He's scared as all get out. He did comment on a wood lean-to with scribe on it."

Parks looked up puzzled, "What did it say?"

"That's what we were going to find out. The Simpson boy can't read a lick. We thought it might be a note from Free."

"I'm going out there, Milt. You stay put for now." Parks rushed down to Horse. "I'll find out what's happened."

"Parks."

Parks jumped up in the stirrup and looked back, "What is it, Milt?"

"This came from the fort while you was away," Milt removed a folded piece of paper from his shirt pocket. "Lieutenant Swafford brought it for you."

Parks reached down and took the paper from the man's outstretched hand. He opened the paper and read the note carefully.

Sir,

We have a need of fifty Indian ponies immediately. Please make way to Fort Riley with mustangs in quick haste.

George A. Custer
Lieutenant Colonel 7th Cavalry

Parks crumpled up the paper and let it drop to the dirt street below. "Tell Lieutenant Swafford, I am engaged in other matters and will not be able to fulfill the lieutenant colonel's request at this time."

Milt stared at the paper on the ground and without looking up said, "There's one more thing, Parks. . . the Simpson boy also said there's a fresh grave out at Free's."

An hour later, Parks stood over the lean-to and read the message from Free. Torn as to his course, he knew the quickest way to the Guadalupes might be along the southern trail. With Horse's endurance and speed, he could be there in two days. But riding south meant Free would be all alone until they met up in the Guadalupes. He read Free's message once more and then he gazed out toward Martha's grave. After several minutes, he lifted the reins back over Horse's head, stepped up in the stirrup and turned the mustang west.

CHAPTER 9

The Comancheria, Texas December 1868

Free rode west into the Comancheria, away from his burned out homestead. Images of his mother consumed his every thought. Her battered face, etched deep into his mind, brought forth a welling of tears and pain in his heart. The anguish was so great that he chose to close his eyes to the world around him and allowed Spirit to walk, trot or gallop as he pleased.

As darkness enveloped the country, his body felt the effects of the saddle and the exhaustion brought on by the passing of his mother. Again and again, the unrelenting call to sleep forced his eyelids to sag, and with each closing, his chin dropped wearily to his chest where his eyes would pop open and startle him awake. After several hours of riding in this state, he surrendered to his body's requirement, dropped his reins, and slid off the saddle to the prairie grass below.

The December morning chill shivered Free awake. He rubbed his eyes and tried to shake the unsettling images he had dreamed from his foggy mind. Relieved to be awake, he viewed Spirit grazing nearby and suddenly realized he lay on the hard ground of the Comancheria. Jerking upright, the previous day's events rushed back in a flood. This was no dream. Now purged of tears, he stood unbound to his grief.

He was unsure of the distance he had traveled into the Comanche land since sorrow had been his only guide. He stared out at the vast open prairie, committed to a singular purpose, the safe return of Clara.

As he rose from the damp ground and dusted his pants, he heard a high-pitched warning from Spirit. Agitated, the roused horse motioned his head up and down and mouthed his bit. Free swiveled his head to the northwest in an attempt to locate the source of the mustang's anxiety. He watched a rider approach at a torrid pace over the horizon.

Free grabbed for his Colt and then reached for Spirit's reins.

"Whoa, Spirit," he spoke to the mustang, "Let's see what this is about."

Fifty yards out, Free heard the rider call, "Comanch! The savages are on the raid!"

Taking heed of the rider's cry, Free topped Spirit just as the approaching horse reined to a stop. Face to face, he saw that the rider was only a boy, probably not more than ten years of age. "What is it, son?"

"Comanch, sir! They're raiding our house back down the Salt Creek! My pa sent me to warn the other families in the settlement line! You best make your way to safety, sir!"

"Who's with your pa?" Free looked back to the northwest.

"Just my ma and two sisters." The boy looked to the south, "I've got to ride, sir."

"Get about it then, son, and good luck." Looking west, Free's thoughts dwelled on Clara and of his commission. After a moment's reflection, he turned Spirit northward and yelled to the departing boy, "I'll be going to help your pa now, son."

Free followed the boy's tracks to the Salt Creek until he heard the clamor of gunfire. He spurred Spirit forward and covered the remaining ground to the siege in little time. From a point fifty yards from the battle, Free pulled reins and stopped Spirit so he could survey the proceedings. A chaotic scene lay in front of him. He saw settlers inside a small frame house encircled by a line of oak pickets. He then heard the distinct roar of two rifles. By the report, it appeared the forted-up settlers fired repeaters.

The Comanche lay entrenched along the west bank of the creek, only two hundred feet or so from the house. Free watched several braves crawl forward each time the settlers reloaded. He figured the Comanche were trying to get close enough to set the house on fire and force the settlers to take the fight outside.

He turned Spirit back east and began a fast ride toward the fortified house. He reckoned it made more sense to enter the pickets on the far side of the Indian positions.

After a quarter mile ride east, he turned Spirit to the west and spurred the mustang hard for the backside of the pickets. Upon reaching the house, he began yelling to the settlers inside, "I'm here to help! Don't shoot!"

A voice from inside hollered, "You best get inside, sir, or be killed by the savages!"

Hidden from the Comanche's view by the house, Free called back to the settlers, "I met your boy on the prairie! I'm here to help, so hold your fire while I make a run on the Indian position!"

"That sounds foolhardy, sir! Please come inside where we might hold the savages at bay!"

"They aim to burn you out! Just let me have a chance!"

"It's your skin! Have at it!" the voice from the house called back.

Free dismounted and pulled the skinning knife from his boot. He made a long slash along his palm and then watched as blood oozed from the cut filling his hand in crimson. He moved to Spirit's rear and pressed his bloodied hand against the mustang's hide. Then he repeated the process on the animal's opposite flank. His task completed, he jumped up in the saddle and maneuvered Spirit to the north. He stopped one hundred yards up the creek from the Comanche position and held his gaze on the fighting below him.

"OK, Spirit, if you've ever run, now is the time." He dropped his hat to the ground, slapped the reins and took spurs to the mustang's flank. Spirit pushed his head into the wind and began a dead sprint down the bank of the creek, running through hanging grapevine and cottonwood branches. Midway to the Comanche attackers, the mustang hit full speed and with powerful strides blazed a path through the landscape. Free felt the mustang's power and whipped the reins hard across the pony's shoulders urging him by the Comanche under a hail of arrows. As he blared by he yipped, "*Marʉaweeka*!" in a booming voice. Free felt certain the bloodied handprint on the mustang's flank and his bare head caught the attention of the Comanche.

From the creek bed came the astonished cries of, "*Cuhtz baví*!" As Kiowa allies, the Comanche knew of the Buffalo brother.

Free heard the shouts and turned Spirit around. He pushed the excited pony back north screaming louder, "*Marʉaweeka*!" a greeting of hello.

The returned shouts of, "*Cuhtz baví*!" once again carried the whole of the creek. The Comanche emerged from their hiding yipping and shaking their bows in the air.

Free counted fifteen braves in paint all standing on the banks of the Salt Creek. In a flash, he turned the mustang and rode toward the warriors. The Indians rushed him with a great clamor and encircled Spirit. Each of the warriors took great pride in touching the bone pipe hanging from the mustang's ear and patting the horse's flank.

Free looked down at the band and struck his chest, "Buffalo brother." He called out.

"*Cuhtz baví*!" The braves echoed.

Free dismounted Spirit and looked at the Comanche around him. The warriors were slender, and all wore a weave of feathers in their hair. "Do any of The People speak English?" he asked.

One warrior stepped forward and spoke,

"*Haa*!"

Free knew a few Comanche words and understood the speaker to say yes.

"What band?"

"Kotsoteka." The brave answered, "You are the buffalo man?"

"*Haa*," Free replied. "And this place is sacred to the buffalo." Free knew the Kotsoteka were one of several bands of Comanche who ranged out of Indian Territory, following the buffalo and calling themselves The People. "If The People fight on this land, the buffalo will go away."

The warrior chief seemed deep in thought at the pronouncement. After several minutes he announced, "I am Mow-way."

Free moved toward the picket gate of the settlers' home with the Comanche following close. When he reached the gate, he made a fist several times causing the blood to flow once more in his palm. He looked to Mow-way and then pressed his bloodied palm onto the picket gate. "The buffalo man asks the great warrior, Mow-way, to leave this place in peace from this time forward."

The chief stared at the bloodied imprint and then nodded his head. "As long as the buffalo are plentiful, the Kotsoteka will honor this place."

"*Ʉra*!" Free smiled.

"*Haa*!" Mow-way answered with a loud whoop and then motioned to his braves. The band walked back to the creek and mounted their ponies. As they rode north, Free heard Mow-way shout back, "*Noo nu puetsuku u punine cuhtz baví*!"

Free understood the chief's message, *I'll see you again, buffalo brother.*

From the rifle cut-out of a shuttered window, Erath Good stared in wonderment at the scene outside. The black cowboy stood face to face with the Comanche chief in front of his picket gate. After several minutes, the cowboy pressed his hand to the front of the picket gate, and the chief nodded as if in agreement. There were a few more words, and then the Indians moved back toward the creek and their ponies.

Satisfied as to the safety of his family, Erath opened the front door and spoke to the stranger outside. "I don't know who you are, Mister, but I can't say I've ever seen the Comanche talked out of a fight before."

"Just lucky, I reckon," Free answered.

"How is it you know the language?" Erath asked.

"I've picked up a few words over time," Free replied.

Erath walked to the picket gate and stared at the bloody print set on the wood. "What's this mean?"

"It means that particular band of Comanche won't be bothering you or your family again."

"Well, I'll be hanged." Erath looked carefully at the man before him. "My name is Erath Good."

"Free Anderson." Free extended his hand. "I'd shake with you, but you might get a bit bloodied."

Erath grabbed Free's hand and shook it with a sturdy grip. "I'd be honored if you'd come inside, Free Anderson. Least I can do is offer you food and drink."

"I appreciate the hospitality, Erath, but I have urgent affairs that need attending," Free replied.

Erath saw a pained look on Free's face, "Please, at least come meet my wife and daughters."

Free looked at the settler and nodded yes. "I would be pleased to do so, Erath."

Free held a hot cup of coffee in both hands and inhaled the dark aroma. Erath Good sat across from him at a small cedar table. "This coffee is a joy to smell, Miss Rebecca." Free looked up at Erath's wife.

"So tell me, Free," Erath asked, "How is it those Comanch listened to you?"

"It's a long story, Erath, and I hate to be rude, but as soon as I finish this coffee, I must be riding out."

"Free, I owe you my life and the lives of my wife and children. If you are heading out toward difficulty, I would be obligated to help."

"Erath, my wife has been kidnapped and my farm burned to the ground by a hard case who goes by Tig Hardy. I would not oblige you to follow into that kind of trouble."

"But with the Comanch gone and the promise not to bother our place again, I insist, Free." Erath's intentions were clear.

"One thing you need know, Erath. The Comanche are not like the Kiowa. They travel in bands, uniting as they see fit for battle. The only thing I can promise you is that band, the Kotsoteka, will not bother you again. I can't speak for any other bands roaming the Comancheria. So you best keep with your own and be watchful everyday. Don't let yourself be caught in the open without a weapon and most of all, Erath, keep a keen eye on your girls. The Comanche can grab a child and be twenty miles away before you know they've gone missing."

The settler nodded and extended his hand. "I still have an obligation to repay you some day, Free."

Free shook the settler's hand and stood, ready to depart. "The only thing I would ask Erath is that you welcome a friend who might ride your way. His name is Parks Scott. If he comes, I would ask you point him to my trail."

"That I will do, Free."

"Mr. Anderson," Rebecca said, "At least carry some dried pork with you." She held out a cloth wrapped with a large portion of meat. "This, I will insist."

Free nodded his head as show of thanks, "Much obliged, Miss Rebecca.

Outside, mounted and ready to press forward, Free bade farewell to the Good family. He cast a long gaze at the two young girls who waved goodbye with overflowing enthusiasm. This was tough country for children to grow up in. He hoped the girls survived the next band of Comanche. Knowing he had done all he could for the Goods, he turned Spirit west and rode toward New Mexico packing an uneasy feeling of being trailed.

CHAPTER 10

The Sand Hills, Texas December 1868

As if by magic, the scrub landscape disappeared. In its stead, a covering of white now engulfed the land. Miles of elongated peaks of sand projected across the horizon. To Clara, it seemed as if all of West Texas had abruptly become a desert. Each time her horse crested one of the sand hills, another rose into view, like waves rolling across the sea.

The all-night ride from *Agua de Mesteño* drained her and left her horse covered in white foam. And now, the careworn animal battled the constant shifting sand in an attempt to move forward. With each step, she felt the horse sink deeper into the loose grains of soil that composed the Sand Hills. Panicked in its attempt to free itself, the horse whinnied and reared back as it clambered against nature's vise-like trap. As the animal fought the sand, Clara noticed a ring of blood forming on her wrists. The knots that Jordie tied to bind her to the saddle had dug deep into her flesh with each movement of the flailing horse.

Clara studied her surroundings with great deliberation. She knew it was important to loose herself from Jordie and find Free before Tig showed up. "Jordie, we need to rest these animals," she pleaded to the rider in front of her.

"I don't know why I let you talk me into this." Jordie turned back to her, "If we stop, Tig will catch up to us. And you can bet he is riding hard on our trail."

"Jordie, it's not going to matter much if we don't rest these horses. If they die, Tig will catch up to us no matter what."

"Dang!" Jordie cursed, Why'd I have to be so stupid!"

"Jordie, you're not stupid!" Clara knew she needed to calm the man. "You made the right move. We just need to rest so we can get away from Tig."

Jordie pulled reins and looked back. "OK! We'll rest. Just shut-up, will ya?"

Thankful that she had managed to get through to Jordie, she nodded her head and held her silence.

"Chase once told me a man could dig down several feet and hit good water here." Jordie stepped from his mount and followed the rope securing the horse behind him. "He said, this is where he would hide out if the law was chasing him." He reached up and untied Clara's hands. "We'll rest here a short while. I figure the quickest way out of the desert is west."

Clara rolled off her mount and knelt in the sand. She placed her hands on the small of her back and rocked back and forth trying to loosen the knots down her spine. She held uneasiness in her stomach and she prayed no harm had come to the baby during the long ride.

"Hold your rein, if your horse takes off out here, you'll have a long walk out."

Clara turned and took the reins from Jordie. "Thanks." She smiled while wrapping the reins securely around her hand. "Do we need to wipe the horses down?" she asked.

"You do what you want. Me? I'm getting some shut-eye." Jordie fell back against the sand hill.

Clara glanced at Jordie. Above his waist hung one pistol and there were no cartridges on the gun belt. She ripped a long patch of cloth from her sleeve and began to wipe the foam from the horse's chest just as she had watched Parks and Free do a hundred times before. She reached as far back under the saddle as she could, and when finished, she glanced back to Jordie. His hat, pulled low over his brow, hid his eyes and he was snoring contentedly. The rope Jordie employed to lead her horse was tied to his boot above the ankle. She walked over to his horse and with little sound, removed the bladder from the saddle. She made special note that the rope around Jordie's ankle tied him to the saddle. Glancing back once more to her sleeping captor, she held quiet. The loudness of his snoring proved the deep state of his rest. With great trepidation, she removed the bunk-roll from Jordie's saddle and then slipped back to her horse.

She removed the stopper from the bladder and poured water down her hand, letting the animal slurp what it could. She knew if she was to make her escape, her horse needed water and rest. After she used half of the water, she took a quick sip and then placed the bladder over her saddle. Looking back to Jordie, she leaned back into the sand and closed her eyes, but instead of sleep, her mind raced feverishly trying to decide what to do next.

After a while, Clara opened her eyes and looked skyward. From their position against the sand hill, she knew the sun would soon move to the opposite side of the bank. When it did, the rays would wake Jordie from his sleep. She studied the surrounding desert and knew the unmoving wind would show any tracks she made while attempting to escape. Anxious and frightened, she also knew this was December and by the look of the northern sky, a cold front was building and might blow in by evening. She rubbed the lightweight fabric of her shirt and knew she would freeze in the desert without more clothing or fire. She reckoned the odds were stacked against her. To ride back northeast out of the desert would put her straight into Tig's path. If she tried to cross the desert toward the southwest, she faced the real possibility of Indians and freezing temperatures. And if she started a fire, Tig, Jordie or the Apaches would know her precise location.

Oh, Free! What should I do? She asked herself, stifling her need to cry out.

A sudden tightness around his boot startled Jordie awake. He could feel sand rushing up his shirt and into his face. He tried to open his eyes but it was useless against the fine particles pelting him relentlessly.

"Sorry, Jordie!" He heard a voice yell.

And then he realized his horse was dragging him across the desert floor. He tried to bend forward at the waist, but the speed at which he was being dragged prohibited the movement. Rolling his head back, he could see the upside down figure of a horse and rider galloping across the sand and away from him.

"What in the tarna—!" he screamed. "I'll kill you for this, Clara!"

His horse, terrified by the counter weight of his body, raced between dunes where the sand had less give. The animal's thunderous hooves rumbled dangerously close to his head. "Stop!" he screamed at the runaway. "Stop, dangit!"

After a quarter mile, Jordie could feel his clothes beginning to shred under the friction of the sand grit. Left with little course of action, he reached down to his gun belt and loosened the leather ring holding his Colt in place. As his body continued to jounce from the desert floor, he took careful aim at the rope binding him to the horse. Holding steady, he squeezed the trigger, but the bullet veered wide of the target. He wrapped both hands around the gun handle, trying to control the shaking, and shot again. Once more, the bouncing sent his bullet wide of the rope. "Hold still!" he cried. In desperation, he pulled the trigger three times in succession. All three bullets were true but not to his target. Almost immediately, the horse stopped and dropped in the desert sand. Three bullets lodged in his chest.

"Blazes!" Jordie screeched.

With his horse dead, Jordie rolled forward and shot again, splitting the rope holding him in place. He untangled himself from the rope, sat up and gasped for breath, spitting sand in great mouthfuls over his tattered shirt. "Gawd darn it!" he cursed.

He felt the rapid beat of his heart pulsing against his temple. Panicked, he hurriedly crawled to the now still horse. He reached for his water bladder and realized it was not on the saddle. Frantic, he searched all around the horse and surrounding sand. He looked back to see if it had fallen during the breakaway. Frustrated, he slapped the saddle with a resounding smack. He reached under the horse to release the girth belt and discovered the empty, leather rifle scabbard. The hard reality that the girl had the water, the rifle and his bunk-roll hit him like a mule's kick. "I'm done in for sure," he muttered.

CHAPTER 11

Nathan Polk's Trading Camp, Texas
December 1868

Sitting on Spirit in a cover of scrub, Free rocked his head to the left and then the right in a slow, deliberate movement. It was a habit formed during his war days to ease tension. A series of snaps and cracks issued from his neck and interrupted the quiet of the day.

Since bidding farewell to the Good family, his soldier instinct had kept his mind on high alert. The occasional snap of a dried prairie grass stalk or the rustle of dried leaves reinforced his suspicion that someone followed his trail, but the stalker remained well hidden. Now as he sat above the rocky shoreline of the *Agua de Mesteño* a more pressing problem presented itself.

He leaned forward over Spirit's neck and surveyed the scene in the trading camp. What appeared to be two border ruffians trampled over the trader's merchandise. Both wore dark dusters that Free figured hid a set of Colt pistols. By all appearances, the men were among the willows.

He looked back west, debating the wisdom of heading into the trading camp. Most likely, Tig supplied here. He was miles from anywhere and Free did not like his odds of riding into the camp alone. The wise thing would be to move on. Still, he reckoned the trader would be able tell him what he needed to know, when Tig arrived and where in the Guadalupes he was headed. With an ample portion of reluctance, Free nudged Spirit with his spurs. From his experience, he had a fair idea of what might happen in the camp, but his mind was set come the hard trail or not. He pressed his tongue against his teeth and issued a clicking sound to the mustang, "Time to go, Spirit," he whispered, "no use in beating the devil around this stump any longer."

"Afternoon." Free, sitting tall, walked Spirit into the trading camp, cautiously announcing his presence to the group.

"Afternoon, stranger." The trader whittled on a piece of driftwood without as much as a glance up. "Something I can do you for?"

Free took a heedful look at the two men sitting several yards away on a large piece of flat rock. Both wore more than a few days' growth of whiskers. The taller of the men wore a coonskin hat on his head. "I'm looking for a friend." Free's words were measured, his gaze fixed on the two men.

"Sorry, mister, I only sell or trade goods here." The trader said, "Information giving seems to only create problems. I know it don't make a man much money." He laughed.

"I'd be willing to pay you fairly for the word," Free proposed. "It's important to me." He looked to the trader.

"Hey, Mr. Colored Man!" One of the ruffians yelled out, "Is that a bangtail you're a'riding?"

Free knew they were referring to the fact that Spirit was an Indian pony. "Pardon me?" Free made note that both men's dusters were buckled behind their Colts.

The man in the coonskin hat stood. "He said is your hoss a bangtail?"

"If you say so." Free answered and then addressed the trader again. "What do you think, Mr. . . ?"

"Polk. Nathan Polk." The trader returned to his whittling,

but he whispered in a low voice, "And I *think* you're about to step off in a hornet's nest, son."

Hearing the trader's whisper, Free refocused his attention on the ruffians. He reminded himself that riding west would have been the smart move. *With whiskey running through them, these two are all-fired for trouble*, he thought.

Both men were on their feet now, and the man in the coonskin hat began to circle behind Spirit with a cocky stride. Free decided his best course was to stay mounted. "I wouldn't get too close, sir. He's been known to make a man bite the ground."

The smaller of the ruffians was now standing directly in front of Free. He pushed his beaver top hat back and called to his friend. "Isham, look who thinks he's the biggest toad in the puddle."

Free put his left spur into Spirit's flank. The horse kicked at Isham forcing the man to jump back toward the river.

"I warned you nicely," Free spoke, his stare fixed on Beaver Hat.

Isham stumbled backward into the water. He looked at his wet boots and laughed aloud. "I'll bet that horse'll burn the breeze. Whataya think, Coy?"

"I'll bet he will." Coy laughed back. "What do you want for him, Mr. Colored Man?"

"I don't think he'll be for sale today." Free spoke with a bravado that belied his predicament. Caught between the two, he could not make a play without catching lead from one of the men.

"Land sakes, man, I guess we'll just take him then." Coy grinned.

"That's what we're gonna do." Isham joined in.

"You aim to shoot a man in the back?" Free yelled out.

"Front, back, it really don't matter to us." Coy laughed. "But we don't want to hit the horse on accident, so why don't you just step down real easy like?"

"That I'll do, boys." Free announced, "You two seem death on for a fight."

Isham and Coy erupted in laughter.

"Didya hear that?" Coy stopped his laughter and snarled, "Git off my horse, mister! Git off now and pull foot!"

Free pushed his boot against the stirrup and stepped down on the mustang's left side. As he lowered from the saddle, he slid his right hand to his gun belt, readying himself to pull the Colt. Calculating as he moved, he decided to shoot Coy first since the man held the better shooting position. As his feet touched the ground, he pushed Spirit's head to the right with his left hand. The motion swung the mustang's rear around and created a shield between him and Isham. Colt in hand, he fired from under Spirit's neck hitting Coy square in the chest.

The man's face showed surprise at the quickness of Free's play. He looked down and clutched his chest as a dark stain began to spread across his shirt.

Without hesitation, Free turned quickly and saw Isham with both hands held high, gripping Colts. Free braced for the bullets but none were forthcoming. *Big mistake, Isham.* He reckoned the ruffian must have set store by Spirit and did not want to shoot through the mustang. The slight delay gave Free the split second he needed to pull the trigger on his Colt. The bullet hit the man with a force that knocked his hat to the ground and spun him to his knees. Free held his Colt on the man and watched as Isham struggled to gain his feet.

"Drop it! And you can vamoose out of here, Isham."

"You can go to blazes!" Isham hollered as he raised his Colts to fire.

You've got more grit than sense. Free pulled the trigger on his Colt twice in rapid succession and watched as Isham fell facedown on the river rock.

"That'll be enough."

Free spun toward the voice and cocked his Colt ready to

fire. Not two feet away, he saw that Nathan Polk held a big fifty on his chest.

"Drop it!" the trader barked. "This Sharps will put a hole the size of a whiskey bottle in a buffalo; just think what it'll do to you!"

"Wait a minute, Mr. Polk! You know I didn't have a choice in the matter!"

"Drop it, I said!" Polk screamed once more, "I don't allow no man to come in and shoot up my camp, especially no colored."

"Mr. Polk, I only—."

"Drop that Colt!" Polk screamed and cocked the Sharps, "I won't be asking you again!"

Free dropped the pistol onto the rocky ground of the riverbank.

"Now, kick that gun toward me!" Polk commanded.

Free flipped the gun with the toe of his boot and watched as it landed between the trader's legs.

"Now, take a seat on the ground and be careful when you do!" Polk reached down, picked up Free's gun, and placed it in his waistband.

"Tell me what kinda information you need that would make you get into a fool's gun play like that?"

Free took a seat on the rocks as ordered. "I'm looking for a man goes by the name, Tig Hardy."

"I thought as much." Polk steadied the Sharps, "What's your business with Tig?"

"You know of him?" Free asked.

"You best let me ask the questions. Now, what's your business with Tig?"

Free stiffened his back. "I aim to kill him."

Polk pushed the gun closer. "That's mighty high talk." He grinned, "Tig might not be as obliging to your goal."

Free reckoned he was wasting precious time. "Mr. Polk, I can't rightly speak to your intentions, but I only came here to seek information. I didn't want trouble; those two ruffians brought that down, and you know that is the truth." He looked up at the trader and started to stand. "And I don't want any trouble with you," he declared.

"It's a little late for that, mister! If Tig doesn't kill you, then those two boys' kin will!" Polk slammed the Sharps against Free's temple and then muttered. "A man signs his own death warrant killing Fischers in this part of the world. Everyone knows they're Comancheros, you damned fool!"

CHAPTER 12

Agua de Mesteño, Texas December 1868

The sound of a wagon on rock brought Free's eyes open. He squinted into the brightness of the day and tried to figure how long he had been unconscious. In front of him, facing the river, Polk was loading merchandise into a Conestoga. Four oxen stood rigged in the neck yokes, and Free observed Spirit tied to the sideboard.

"Polk?" Free shouted, the words caused his head to ache and his eyes to close. "What's going on?"

"Winter's fixin' to set in. Time to pack up and leave."

"Well, you're not taking my mustang with you," Free declared. He tried to gain his feet, but his limbs were still shaky.

"I don't think you have much say in the matter." Polk tossed the remaining two buffalo hides into the wagon's bed, "None at all."

Free struggled to his feet and staggered toward the trader. "You hold on, Polk! I said you're not leaving with my horse!"

The trader turned and backhanded Free across the face. The blow sent him reeling with Polk in close pursuit. As Free felt his legs give way, he caught a blur of tan racing toward the trader's back.

Polk lifted his hand to strike once more when the Kiowa dog appeared. The dog leapt and tore into the trader's arm, causing Polk to fall to the ground, screeching in surprise.

"What the—!" Polk tried to roll his hands around his head

for protection. “Get him off me!” he cried, “Please! Get him off me!”

Still woozy, Free stood still, knowing the better of getting between a fighting dog and his prey. “Hey!” he screamed over the dog’s madness and then gave a shrill whistle. The crazed dog was oblivious and tore at Polk’s forearm swinging the helpless man’s limb back and forth in a frenzy. “Hey!” Free screamed again, “Easy now! Easy, boy.”

The dog gradually slowed his movements but kept his jaws clamped on Polk’s arm. The animal looked up at Free with his mouth pulled taut and a fair amount of the trader’s flesh in his mouth.

Free walked over and spoke to the dog, “Easy. Good job, boy. Good dog.” He reached out tentatively and patted the dog’s head. “So you were the *someone* following my trail.”

“Get him off me!” Polk continued to scream, as a river of blood flowed down his wrist.

Free fixed a hard stare into Polk’s eyes. “You best calm down and keep your tone civil, Mr. Polk, or I’ll let this dog eat you alive.”

Polk nodded in defeat. “Just get him away from me,” he whispered.

“I’ll do that right after you answer my questions,” Free stated sharply. “I ought to shoot you for hitting me with that Sharps.”

“I’ll do whatever you want. Just get this dog off me.” Polk sobbed.

Free patted the dog’s head once more and then spoke to Polk, “I prefer to let the dog keep his grip until I get my answers, Mr. Polk.”

“Just hurry.”

“When did Tig pass through here?”

“He’ll kill me if I tell you.” Polk pulled his face away from the dog.

The dog scooted back on his haunches and pulled tighter

on the trader's arm. The animal issued a low growl to show his intent.

"The dog's going *to kill* you if you don't tell." Free stated matter-of-factly, "And you know what, Polk, it doesn't matter to me. I'll leave you with this dog right now, and I'll move up the trail with your wagon in tow."

"All right! All right! Tig was here two days ago, toward sundown. He bought some whiskey and dried beef, and then he left. And that's all I know!"

"Did he have anybody with him?"

"He come alone. We shared a bottle, and then he left."

"You didn't see a woman?"

"I'm telling you he rode into camp same as you. There weren't a soul with him. And that's the truth."

Free gazed down the trail. His mind digested Polk's words. *Tig was alone. Where was Clara?* he wondered. *Had she had managed to escape? That has to be it*; *I won't believe otherwise*, he told himself. And if she had escaped, then he needed to find her before Tig. "What's the quickest way to the Guadalupes?"

Polk grimaced in pain. "The quickest or the safest?"

"The quickest," Free said.

"You'd need to ride south toward the Sand Hills. Mister, please get this dog off me," Polk pleaded.

"How many days' ride?" Free asked.

"On your horse, one day." Polk grimaced.

"You think Tig would go that way?"

"Only a fool would head that way."

Free stood and walked to the wagon. He looked under the driver's seat and found his Colt. "I'll be taking my Colt."

Polk nodded.

"And the Sharps." Free walked to Spirit and untied the pony. "You have a protest with any of that?" he asked Polk.

"None." The trader frowned, "None at all."

"Good," Free said dryly and then lifted the tobacco pouch

from his neck. “When we’re done here, you might want to doctor that wound, Mr. Polk.” Free cut a plug from the tobacco and pushed it into the back of his jaw, “A dog bite can leave a man with the fever.”

He replaced the pouch, stepped up on Spirit and called to the dog. “Let’s go, Dog.”

The dog issued a guttural growl, shook the trader’s arm violently for good measure and then released his prey.

Free rode Spirit out of the camp and up the far bank. As he crested the bluff overlooking the camp, he hollered out, “Fair warning to you, Mr. Polk. If I ever see you again, I aim to repay you for the knock on the head.”

CHAPTER 13

Apache Seep, The Sand Hills, Texas
December 1868

As twilight emerged, Clara rode hard for a small grouping of shin oak. The chaparral grew in a tight clump below the convergence of two sand dunes. She took the beckoning trees as sanctuary from the building north wind. Urging the horse forward into the tightly wound tree branches, she found a small clearing laced with squawbush. A small oval of stones lay at the far edge of the refuge. Nudging her horse toward the rocks, she saw a seep of clear water pooled inside the aggregate. Energized, she bounded from the horse and for the first time in days exhaled a breath of relief.

With only a few minutes of usable light left in the sky, a fire was the first priority to surviving the night. Frantic, she began to strip the brown leaves found near the base of each tree. With the approach of winter, the deciduous plant yielded a bounty of the dead foliage. Using her shirt as a basket, she gathered a garment full of the plant material and dumped it on the ground near the seep. Hurrying against the encroaching darkness, she began snapping dead twigs from off the trees. Securing a large bundle of the kindling, she rushed back to the seep and dropped to her knees. She worked in great haste and arranged six of the largest rocks around the dead leaves, then glanced skyward at the last vestige of light. She fumbled in her shirt pocket looking for the safety match Jordie had stuck there days earlier. Deep in the pocket, the Lucifer lay hidden among the dust and lint. "Where are you?" she shouted aloud. Then her fingers felt the slender wooden stick. Clumsily, she rolled the match up the side of her pocket and pulled it into view. "Please work," she uttered in desperation.

In a careful and calculated movement, she raked the head of the match against one of the stones and watched the sparks fly. Instantly, the pungent smell from the phosphorous emission filled her nose. Using her free hand as a mantle, she delicately put the match to the dried leaves. The acrid smell of smoke plumed upward, followed by a crackle of fire that caused the pile to glow orange. As the flames devoured the leaves, she carefully added the small kindling twigs one at a time. Within minutes, a humble but fueled fire lit her hideout.

The dim light put off by the fire yielded a sense of security and propelled her toward the next chore. Her horse needed tending to. Time was pressing to remove the saddle and rub the animal down before the freezing temperatures of the night settled over the desert. Left to soak in its sweat, the animal could die of pneumonia by morning.

She grabbed the lead rein and tied the horse to the trunk of a shin oak. Reaching under the animal, she released the girth strap from its ring and yanked the saddle toward her. As the saddle dropped to the ground, the horse issued a series of warning snorts, its eyes opened wide in fear. From behind, the heavy rustling of breaking shin oak branches caused her to throw her head around, uncertain as to the cause.

Out of the darkness, a man crashed through the small forest of oak and landed face down in front of Clara. From his shirtless back emerged two arrows, and the man's gaunt appearance told her he had traveled far to arrive at the seep. She rushed over, grabbed his arms and pulled him toward the light of the fire. Running back to her horse, she pulled the rifle from its ring and held a cautious gaze toward the entrance of the oaks, hoping no Indians had followed.

Minutes later, certain of their security, she returned to the man and began to examine his wounds. The first arrow lay embedded below the shoulder in the soft muscle of his lower back. The second arrow was a few inches to the right of his backbone. The arrows belonged to Apaches, as each bore three fletched feathers from a red hawk. Looking at each wound, she feared the flint arrowhead, bound by deer sinew and mixed with the man's blood, had expanded and tightened to the shaft. It would take some effort to extract the arrow without breaking the tip.

"Mister?" she whispered. "Can you hear me?"

The man moaned and nodded his head.

"I'm going to help, but what I have to do is going to hurt you real bad. Promise me you can stay quiet. Do you understand?"

The man nodded once more and moved his forearm under his mouth.

"The only way this arrow is coming out whole will be if I shake it back and forth to widen the wound. If I don't, the flint shoulders will never release. I'm truly sorry."

The man bit down on his forearm and nodded once more.

Clara gripped the shaft with both hands and rocked the arrow back and forth violently, watching the man as she proceeded. A vein grew large on his forehead and beads of sweat formed on his reddening face. Realizing the man's extreme hurt, she rocked harder and then standing, pulled with all of her strength on the arrow. The man gave a muffled cry as the flinthead tore through muscle and skin on its exit. He moaned once more and then passed out from the pain.

Clara ripped her other sleeve and dipped the cloth into the seep. After wringing out the dampened material, she wrapped it around an oak branch and held it over the fire. When the water evaporated, she removed the cloth and laid it across the wound as a poultice. With the man passed out, she hurried to work on the second arrow.

An hour later, she used Jordie's blanket to cover the resting man and then finished wiping down her horse. Alone and miserable, she rested against the saddle with the Winchester across her chest. As she listened to the night sounds, she realized her prospect of heading west and away from Jordie was now at a standstill.

CHAPTER 14

The Sand Hills, Texas December 1868

Tig worked his horse between the dunes of the Sand Hills, looking for any sign of horse tracks in the shifting soil. The ground exhibited the fresh markings of a ringtail lizard. By the zigzag movement of the tracks, the speedy little reptile was probably on the run from a burrowing owl. He leaned over the left side of his mount and picked out the faint shape of a print that could belong only to a shod horse. He rose in the saddle and surveyed the desolate landscape before him. If Jordie was between dunes, he might never find him. He took his gaze back to the track and walked his horse west, following what he could of the wind blown trail.

Several miles into the wasteland, he found depressions that appeared to be tracks leading up one of the larger dunes. From the size of the indentions, he reckoned the horses fought hard against the sliding sand as they tried to cross over the hill. *Lucky me*, he mused. The struggle had left so large a depression that the previous evening's winds did not erase them completely. Tig brushed the reins slightly over his horse's neck and urged the beast over the mound ahead.

As his horse crested the hill, the backside of a man on his knees came into view. The figure threw great handfuls of sand into the air as he dug frantically in the white sand. Next to the man in a darkened stain of blood lay a dead horse.

"Hello, Jordie." Tig removed his hat and scratched his

hairline, "Appears your luck keeps heading downhill."

Jordie turned in a start at the voice. Shocked, he gasped for breath at the sound of the man he feared most. "Tig," he said weakly. "Am I glad to see you."

Tig set his hat back on his head. "Are you now?" He narrowed his eyes and spat to the ground. "Why's that?"

Jordie stood and faced Tig. He began to crawfish in a zigzag movement down the sand valley. "I dunno, Tig, I just am."

Tig moved the horse forward as the scared creature in front of him continued to back away. "You never were a smart one, Jordie."

"That's me for sure, Tig. I never had a lick of sense." Jordie stammered as his retreat slowly garnered speed, "Not a lick."

"You ran out on Chase and you ran out on me!" Tig thundered.

"It wasn't like that, Tig." Jordie threw up his hands in an attempt to placate the devil in front of him.

"It was the woman, Tig. It was her idea. I know I should have never listened to her . . .," Jordie forced a weak smile. "But it won't happen again, Tig. I promise it won't."

Tig pushed his horse to within a foot of his prey. "I know it won't, Jordie. Where's the woman?" he hissed.

Jordie stumbled as Tig's horse bumped him. He fell and then regained his feet quickly. "I don't know, Tig." His voice quivered, "She bushwhacked me she did."

Tig continued his relentless forward push on the cowering rabbit of a man in front of him. "Ambushed you?" An evil grin formed on his lips. "Is that a fact?"

"Yes, that's what happened, Tig. I was trying to catch some shut-eye, and she bushwhacked me." Jordie turned his shoulders and looked at the endless valley of sand surrounding him. Huge mounds of white kept him penned, trapped by the approaching Tig. He glanced back, a sheen of sweat on his face. "I know I messed up, Tig, but let me make it up to you," he pleaded.

"Where's the woman, Jordie?" Tig settled his right hand

near his Colt.

Jordie recoiled, "I dunno, Tig. I'm sorry, I just don't know." He began to cry. "I'm just a dummy like you said, Tig. I didn't mean to mess up. I didn't mean to." Tears began to roll down his cheeks.

"Appears you're on the *camino del muerte*, Jordie."

"What's that mean, Tig?" Jordie wiped at his cheeks with his shirtsleeve. "That's a funny word for sure."

"It's what the Mexicans call the way of death." Tig smiled broadly.

"No, Tig! Now just hold on!" Jordie screamed and then broke to his left. He began a desperate run up the large dune, but the shifting sand grabbed at his feet and tripped him face first into the hill. He rolled over in a panic with a layer of white painted across his face. "Please, Tig." He held his hands in front of his face, "Please."

The solitary gunshot reverberated throughout the Sand Hills. Tig figured the woman, wherever she was, should have heard it. He hoped she did. He wanted her to pack the same fear Jordie carried before he died. He wanted her to dread knowing that Tig Hardy was coming for her.

Clara thought the new day was forever in starting. As the sun finally rose over the shin oak stand, she laid a piece of heated oak bark on the man's wounds. The heat startled him awake.

"Lay still," she said. "The bark will help draw out any poison."

The man lay on his stomach and looked up. "Is this heaven or the other?"

Clara laughed aloud. "It's a little of each."

"I don't suppose you have any grub? It's been a week since I last ate."

"I have a piece of hard tack that you're welcome to." She

removed the hard bread from a white cloth. "It might take a few minutes of soak to be able to pull at it."

"Believe me, Ma'm. I'd take any nourishment right now."

Clara nodded in understanding and handed the hard tack to the man. "What's your name?" she asked.

"Robert Armstrong McCaslin."

"Well, Mr. McCaslin, my name is Clara Anderson."

"If I might inquire, Ma'm, what's a woman doing out in this God-forbidden country by herself?"

"It's a long story, too long to tell right now, Mr. McCaslin. But the short of it is we need to get you well, because there's a man trailing me that can only mean no good for you if we're caught up to."

"I'm fit as a fiddle," McCaslin said right before he passed out again.

Reluctantly, Clara extinguished their fire. She couldn't take the chance that the smoke would be smelled or seen by Jordie or Tig. She poured handfuls of sand on the flame to avoid smoke. When the fire was out, she buried the entire rock circle in sand in the hope that the chaparral looked as it did the night she rode in. She knew Mr. McCaslin would never be able to keep up in his condition and Tig couldn't be that far behind. A hiding spot seemed the best solution, and much as she hated to do so, she had to let the horse go. If they were lucky, Tig and Jordie might pursue the animal's trail. If not, she did have the Winchester.

Clara had finished cinching the saddle around the horse's belly when the sound of a lone gunshot rode the wind into the chaparral. It was hard to tell the direction from which the gunfire came, but it did not seem far away. Anxious, she led the horse out of the shin oak and with a shout and a hard slap of her hand sent her best means of escape galloping toward the southwest.

CHAPTER 15

Agua de Mesteño, Texas December 1868

The war whoops of Comanche raiders filled the prairie outside of *Agua de Mesteño*. Parks held his ear into the north wind and tried to ascertain the distance to the fight. Unsure as to the identity of the war party's victims, he turned Horse toward the commotion and spurred the mustang toward the sounds of the engagement.

As he rode up a small plateau overlooking the river, he came upon a scene of bedlam. Below him, a band of fifteen Comanche laid siege to a Conestoga wagon. The driver of the wagon stood behind the driver's seat, opposite the attacking warriors. Behind the man, two bodies lay dead on the bank of the river. The Comanche, only twenty feet from the prairie schooner, fired arrows in salutation. The man returned their fire with a Colt pistol.

Parks dismounted and grabbed his Winchester as he rolled off Horse. He found a dead tree limb near the edge of the plateau and dropped to his stomach behind the log. Levering the rifle, he sent a rapid succession of cartridges toward the marauders, intent on giving the impression that more than one man occupied the high ground. He emptied the rifle in less than a minute.

The Comanche looked in his direction and shook their bows at him with spirited yells of, "Yellow boy!" The Indian name for the feared rifle.

"I'll protect you as best I can from here!" Parks hollered to the man below.

"Any help is much appreciated!" the man called back. "I'm out of ammo, and I'm carrying an arrow in my leg!"

Parks pulled cartridges from his belt and began a frantic reload as the Comanche hurried from the scrub cover to the wagon. Within seconds, a group of seven braves had crossed the landscape and pounced on the hapless man.

Parks managed to load only three cartridges before needing to scatter the Indians off their victim. With military precision, he fired into the crowd of Indians, hitting two of the braves.

He began to load anew. He watched as two of the Comanche unhooked the oxen and used the great beasts as cover to depart to the north. Two more of the group gathered their dead and followed the oxen. Parks shot three more times toward the fleeing band. With the Indians back in the scrub, he returned his gaze to the wagon. The man lay face down on the far side of the schooner. One of the Comanche, his face hidden by the sideboard, held a knee in the man's back. In horror, Parks watched as the brave pulled the man's head up and deftly made a quick slice with a long knife. The wagon owner's screams filled the land as the brave pulled hard on the man's scalp and removed it from his head. The Comanche leapt off the man's back and began a rapid sprint for the safety of his band. The warrior shouted and screamed, shaking the bloody scalp as he ran.

Parks drew a bead on the fleeing warrior and placed a well-aimed bullet to his back, sending the Indian head over heels to his death.

Rising from his position, Parks jumped on Horse and spurred the mustang down the incline, firing the Winchester into the scrub as he rode.

Horse sent a splay of water upward as he galloped through the river stream. Parks directed the mustang to the far side of the wagon and found the man attempting to sit up.

"We need to make cover!" he yelled, "I'm not so sure this bunch is gone!"

The man pulled himself up with one hand, the other hand pushed against his forehead to keep the skin from falling down around his face. "Whataya got in mind?"

"Move around the wagon! I'm going to pull her over!" Parks looped his rope over one of the sideboard hooks and then positioned Horse on the opposite side of the Conestoga. "Watch out!" he called and then encouraged the mustang to back up toward the stream.

The wagon flipped in a resounding crash. The angle of the creek bed caused the wooden transport to roll once, landing with its wheels skyward.

"Grab cover!" Parks yelled to the man.

With his back pressed hard against the wagon's wheels, Parks began pushing cartridges into the Winchester. He knew it was vital to load a full magazine in the repeater. As he forced the shells into the gun, he looked over to the wounded man. "Name's Parks Scott," he offered.

"Nathan Polk," the man replied. "I'm a trader who's set camp here for ten years and never once had savages attack. I always made sure to give the Comanche their beads and beef, and this is how that crazy Mow-way pays a man back. I 'spect it has to do with those two dead Comancheros over there."

Parks threw a glance to the two dead bodies. "As soon as I know those Comanche are gone, I'll tend to your leg." He glanced back over his shoulder into the scrub, "They might not be so quick to leave since the brave who lifted your scalp lies dead just beyond us."

Polk, held his forehead skin up with his left hand and stared at the dead Comanche brave. "I aim to retrieve my top-notch," he stated matter-of-factly.

"You don't carry a rifle?" Parks asked suspiciously.

"It was stolen only yesterday." Polk continued to look at his scalp fluttering in the breeze.

"Stolen? You were robbed?"

"That I was. A colored fellow bushwhacked me in this very spot." Polk turned back and pointed toward the ruffians. "Same fella killed those two as well."

"What did this fellow look like?" Parks asked.

"He was tall, muscular and mean as a mother coyote. He had a dog with him who took to my arm." Polk held out his right arm, allowing the loose forehead skin to fall over his eyes.

"This fellow have a name?"

"None that he offered. But he rode a marked Indian pony."

"Marked you say?" Parks slid closer to the man.

Polk pushed the loose skin against his forehead once more. "Yes sir, the beast was marked with an Indian pipe through the ear. That's a spirit sign they say."

Parks pointed the Winchester at Polk. "That man is a friend of mine, Polk! And I'll bet a day's pay; the bushwhacking was the other way around!"

"You're wrong! That colored bushwhacked me I tell you!"

"Where is he?" Parks demanded.

"I don't know! It ain't my job to keep up with every low-life that hits the trail!"

Parks shoved the rifle barrel in Polk's chest. "Polk, I rode into a heap of Comanche today to save your sorry old hide, and all you owe me as debt is the truth. Now, I'm only going to ask you once more, where's my friend?"

Polk swallowed hard and gazed down at the Winchester. "All right!" he shouted. "Your friend is headed for the Sand Hills. He said he was looking for Tig Hardy."

"You know Hardy?" Parks asked.

"I know enough to stay out of his affairs."

"How long ago did my friend leave?"

"Yesterday in the afternoon, and that's all I know."

"Was Hardy here before?" Parks asked.

"Yeah, he rode in two days earlier than your friend."

"What about the woman?"

"I'll tell you like I told your friend; Tig Hardy rode into this camp alone."

"He didn't have a woman with him?"

"He was alone. He rode in alone, and he rode out alone. I don't know anything about a woman."

Parks was baffled. *Where was Clara?* Parks' first order of business was to get to Free. From his war days, he knew a man going into a fight with anger set in his mind made mistakes. He needed to be there when Free confronted Hardy. He looked back toward the scrub, "I aim to treat your leg and bandage your head, Polk. After that you're on your own."

"Wouldn't expect anymore." Polk spoke through his teeth. "But I would be obliged to some of your Colt cartridges."

Parks threw a hard look at Polk. "I think I'll be keeping all my cartridges, Polk. If you need ammo, you can take it off those two over there." He nodded his head toward the two ruffians.

The landscape quieted by late afternoon. Parks reckoned the Comanche were satisfied with the oxen as reward and decided to depart the area. As he scanned the scrub once more for any movement an ironic smile came to his face. Somewhere out on the plain, the body of the brave who scalped Polk was missing along with Polk's scalp.

"Appears your top notch has gone missing, Polk." Parks motioned to the ground outside the wagon.

"What?" Polk scanned the prairie. "How the—"

"You best be careful out here alone; those braves could sneak up on a man in his sleep and cut his throat."

Polk swallowed hard. "But look at my wagon, it's all busted up from you turning it over and my oxen are gone! How the blazes am I supposed to get out of here?"

"I figure you'll be riding shank's mare back to civilization, Polk. And that's probably better than you deserve."

"How'd you arrive to that notion?" Polk replied with agitation in his voice.

"Because you're still holding air in your lungs." Parks mounted Horse and started toward the river stream. He was at least a day back of Free; the only way he could make up the time was to race the mustang all night. He reached down and patted the horse's neck. "It is time to run, Horse," he said.

In perfect understanding, Horse snickered, kicked his hind legs, and galloped up the plateau, south toward the Sand Hills.

CHAPTER 16

Near Lost Creek, Texas December 1868

A myriad of stars flickered in the moonless December sky. Free lay on his back in the shadow of a dying fire and watched as an occasional shooting star blazed across the heavens. The approaching nightfall waylaid the prospect of journeying any further. It was just too dangerous.

With barely enough daylight left to set up camp, Free stopped outside the Sand Hills near Lost Creek. Fatigued, he unsaddled Spirit and gave the mustang a good rub, then built a small fire in the wallow of a wild hog. Right before nightfall, he had the good fortune to kill a jackrabbit in the scrub. He skinned the long-eared beast and roasted it on a stick over the fire. When the rabbit was fully cooked, he ate his fill, grateful for the fresh meat and protein.

The Kiowa dog anxiously paced back and forth twenty yards to his north. After leaving *Agua de Mesteño*, the dog had kept a safe distance and followed Spirit to the present campsite. Watching as the rabbit cooked, he fidgeted, first standing and then sitting, salivating for a share of the rabbit bounty. When a fair portion of one hindquarter came his way, he caught the meat in mid-air and swallowed the morsel in one bite.

Afterward, with his stomach filled, he remained vigilant to the West Texas night's orchestra. Listening to the music of the coyote and screech owl, he instinctively joined in the harmony with his own howls and yips. Only after Free lay on his back did the dog take to the ground, placing his head between outstretched paws and keeping a watchful eye on the trail leading north.

Free had used the day's saddle time to rethink his plan of action. In retrospect, he felt sure Clara was alive and with Hardy. If the outlaw meant to kill her, he would not have left the message about the Guadalupes. Free had encountered the Tig Hardys of the world before, and he found these men incapable of valuing life. They killed at the slightest provocation, and the killings were always justified in their own distorted way of thinking. No, Tig would keep Clara alive, of this Free was now sure. *He wants her to watch me die first*, he thought.

Most likely, Hardy had left her tied up when he visited the trader's camp. That had to be the reason why Polk was adamant that Tig rode in alone, he concluded. His gaze caught another flaming streak light the sky. The split second flare brought back a rush of memories. He remembered sitting on the cold Missouri ground outside the slave quarters where he and his Mother would watch shooting stars race across the winter sky. *Those are lucky stars, son.* Her voice came alive in his head. *Make a wish before they burn out and that wish will come true someday.*

He gazed intently into the sky and waited. And when another star blazed through the heavens, he quickly offered his wish. A wish for Clara and their child and a safe reunion. With the wish completed he slumped, his eyelids were heavy and he desperately needed sleep. But no matter his tiredness, the thought of Clara with child and alone in the desert would make sure that what rest he did get would be fitful.

An hour before dawn, in the gray time between darkness and light, the low growl of the dog roused Free from a restless night. He lay still and listened to the surrounding prairie; a strange silence had spread over the land. Although all seemed quiet and calm, something had the dog riled. Free reached behind his head and pulled the Henry from its scabbard. He rose from his bedroll and levered the rifle in one continuous movement.

The dog rose with him and began a warning growl toward the charcoal prairie to the north. In between the increasingly deeper barks, the dog held his nose high into the morning's approaching dawn, agitated by someone or something beyond the fringe of the camp. Free reckoned this was more than just a skunk or armadillo scavenging for insects. The dog's racket foretold trouble.

He moved to Spirit while keeping his vision on the northern skyline. He reached down and pulled hard on an oak peg that kept the mustang staked during the previous evening. "Easy, Spirit," he whispered.

The mustang eyed the dog and mimicked the animal's aggression, snickering and bouncing his head up and down. Free grasped Spirit's bridle and turned the mustang's head toward the west. He let the animal's body act as a shield between him and the coming danger. In total concentration, he laid the Henry gently across the mustang, using the horse's ample back as a gun rest. He stared down the rifle's sight and watched as the grayness gradually turned to daylight.

As if on command, the Kiowa dog broke north sprinting at full speed toward the still unseen intruder. Far beyond Free's sight, but within hearing range, the dog ratcheted up his aggression with a warning that told the trespasser to stay away. Free visualized the dog circling the interloper, showing his teeth, ready to defend his territory.

Looking beyond the pale, Free saw the outline of a figure, dark against the northern sky. He closed his left eye and focused down the sight, letting his finger linger near the trigger.

"Is this your dog, Sergeant?" A familiar voice hollered over the incessant yapping. "He's full of vinegar, that's for sure."

Free smiled, relieved at his friend's voice. "He'll eat you alive, Parks."

Now in plain view atop Horse, Parks walked the mustang in a meandering gait toward the camp.

"Com'on, dog!" Free slapped at his thigh, "Com'on, boy! It's OK!" He looked at Parks and said, "You're a welcome sight."

Parks pulled reins on Horse several feet from Free. "I feel like I've tasted most of the land between here and The Flats."

Free walked toward Horse and rubbed the animals jaw. "I knew you'd come, no matter what." He looked up at Parks.

Parks dismounted and used his hat to dust his pants. "I'm sorry about your mother, Free. She was a good woman and I loved her as family."

Free swallowed hard and a tear dotted his eye. "Thanks, Parks."

Parks set his hat back on his head. "And I feel as bad as a man possibly could. I have a sense that much of the blame is my fault for riding us down to Fort Concho . . . maybe none of this would have happened if I hadn't shot that cowboy . . ."

"I won't hear any of that, Parks. There's only one man who is due blame in this matter and he's somewhere out there in the desert among those dunes." Free searched the vast sea of sand in front of them and tried to discern any movement.

Parks stared out at the now brightly lit morning sand with a determined look. "I can't say what I'd do in your boots, but I can tell you this, I'm here to help with whatever it is you've decided."

Free pointed into the endless white of the Sand Hills, "They're out there somewhere, Parks. My Clara and Hardy. And Parks, Clara's with child."

"Clara's pregnant?" Parks turned, stunned by what he heard.

"That's what my mother told me right before she died."

Parks walked over to Free and laid a hand on his friend's shoulder. "He wants us first, Free, and he needs her alive to bait us to him."

"Doesn't matter. Either way, Tig Hardy owes me a debt." Free stared at Parks with blank eyes. "A debt that can only be paid one way."

Free's words caused Parks to shiver, sending a chill the length of his backbone. He knew there was nothing more he could possibly say to his friend. His mind was set, and no matter Hardy's crimes, in Texas the law did not recognize an ex-slave's right to justice. Free was prepared to ride a desperate trail, even knowing there would be hard retribution to follow.

Free turned away from the Sand Hills and walked toward the campfire. "I know you've ridden through the night, Parks. You best grab some shut-eye. When you're rested, we'll move through the desert and up into the Guadalupes."

CHAPTER 17

The Apache Seep, Texas December 1868

Clara hurried back into the scrub. She knew it was urgent to get McCaslin on his feet and out of the seep. Letting the horse go was a risky move and she prayed her action had not cost the both of them their lives. But deep inside, she knew the chance of outrunning Tig and Jordie on one horse was a fool's folly.

"Mr. McCaslin." She pushed gently on the sleeping man's shoulder. "Mr. McCaslin, you need to wake up!"

"Huh?" McCaslin, startled, tried to rise, but a stabbing pain along his spine forced him back to the ground. His emaciated figure, shirtless and welted by the ordeal made him seem helpless and small. "What is it?" He looked wide-eyed at Clara.

"We need to move. You must get up. We need to cross over the dune behind us."

"Is someone here?"

"Not yet. But just minutes ago I heard a gunshot." She placed her hand on the man's forehead to check for fever. "The men following me may be close. We need to move now!"

"Help me up!" McCaslin placed both hands behind himself and pushed against the sand.

Clara grabbed McCaslin's forearm and helped pull the man to his feet. "Good, now let's hurry." Reaching down, she grabbed the Winchester with her right hand while supporting McCaslin with her left. "Through here," She pressed her back against the dense brush of the scrub oaks, creating an opening so the wounded man could squeeze through. "We need to get on the other side of that dune." She pointed to a massive sand hill fifty feet or higher thirty feet in front of them.

McCaslin exhaled a low whistle as he stared at the formidable mound of sand. "This may take me awhile," he mumbled.

"We don't have that kind of time!" Clara said urgently, "We need to go quickly!"

The morning sun reflected waves of light off the mountainous sand dunes in the sand hills. The resulting whiteness spread evenly across the desert and blinded any unfortunate human left to wander in the desolation.

"Blazes!" McCaslin huffed. "I can't see that we've made much progress, Clara."

"Just keep trying, please!" She held McCaslin's upper arm with her right hand. Her left hand used the Winchester as support in the constantly sliding sand.

"It seems for every step we take, most of this hill slides down around us," the wounded man complained.

"Fight the sand, Mr. McCaslin; I don't intend to die out in this desert!" She spoke with authority.

"There are men riding here that aim to kill me! And that means they will kill you too! So, I need for you to stop fussing and help me get you up this hill!"

Her urgency and fear got his attention. McCaslin stuck his right hand into the sand and began to push against the dune. He hopped in short bursts up the mound gumming the whole way, "This is some way for a man to spend Christmas Eve."

Christmas Eve. Clara stopped abruptly. *I was going to tell Free about the baby today.*

"Clara, are you OK?" McCaslin turned back.

"Yes, I'm fine." She began moving once more, "That's it. We can do it." She spoke with encouragement as she rushed to keep up with the energized McCaslin. "We're almost there."

Several minutes later, they crested the giant pile of sand and fell exhausted on the opposite side.

Clara's heart pounded wildly in her chest, but without hesitation, she rose at once and slid down the giant mound.

"Where are you going Clara?"

"I've got to clean up our trail," she yelled.

Rolling down the white hill in an avalanche of sand, she placed both hands behind her and used them to break her free-fall. She came to a stop at the bottom of the dune in a spray of sand, leapt to her feet and sprinted for the seep, careful to stay in the same tracks she and McCaslin had used in their exit.

Inside the dense forest, she grabbed the bedroll and bladder and tossed both over her shoulder. She neared the fire pit and spied the ripped sleeve she had used to wipe down the horse. She picked it up and shoved it into her front pocket. Taking a final look at the camp, she pushed her way back through the scrub and stopped outside to break off several small limbs.

Hastily, she backpedaled toward the dune, using the leafy branches to sweep away any sign of footprints left by their struggle to climb the mound. "With the wind blowing across the dune behind me, our tracks should be unnoticeable," she called out.

"You are one smart lady!" McCaslin yelled to her.

"Mr. McCaslin, look back east, do you see any sign of riders?" she hollered.

"Nothing!" Robert called back.

"Good," Clara muttered and then began the arduous backward ascent up the steep hill of sand.

Clara reached the top of the mound and searched the

horizon in all directions for any sight of movement. She held a tight grip on the Winchester, ready to use the rifle if necessary.

"Can you shoot that Winchester?" McCaslin asked.

"I'll do OK. You're not worried about my aim, are you?" Clara asked.

"It's not that, Clara," McCaslin offered. "I can see you are more than able to take care of yourself. But if you have never shot at a man before, there might be some reluctance when you finally set that sight on a human target."

Clara stared out onto the white rolling landscape. She understood Robert's concern, but there was no way she would submit to Hardy's custody again. The baby in her stomach required that. "I promise you, Mr. McCaslin, if the occasion arises to shoot, there will not be any hesitation on my part."

McCaslin reckoned not and offered a wide smile. "I can see that now, Clara. And if it ain't being too nosy, what could you possibly have done that would cause men to trail you so far out in this bone-infested desert?"

Clara glared at the man and issued a thin smile across her lips,

"I could ask the same of you."

"Fair enough." He grinned, "I owe you my story, that's a fact, after all, you did save my life. I was working with a government survey team out of Fort Sumner. About two weeks ago we finished our work and camped just north of here below Antelope Ridge. Before daylight, a band of twenty Apaches attacked the camp, killing six of the eight of us outright. My brother and I survived the fight only because I managed to catch one of the horses the Indians had scattered. The two of us hightailed it out of camp riding to beat the devil."

"And the Apaches didn't follow?" Clara asked.

"One thing about the Apaches, Clara, they love a good game. They sent out a small band to hunt us. It was truly something to watch. Two braves rode on horseback and two others followed by running behind the horses, holding on to their tails."

Clara remembered Parks telling them an Apache could run seventy miles a day on foot and never take a hard breath."

McCaslin continued, "They followed us that way for miles shooting arrows at us the whole time. They shot us and the poor horse full of arrows. We managed to put another mile between us before the horse fell. And my brother, Jim . . . well, he walked as best he could for maybe another mile before he died. I staggered on foot for I don't know how long before I ran into your camp."

"And the Apaches?" Clara asked.

"I don't know. Maybe they stopped to celebrate their victory. Six scalps back at the camp and most likely Jim's later must have satisfied the bloody savages." McCaslin stared without expression into the distant desert.

Clara looked down at the sand. "I'm sorry Mr. McCaslin. I didn't mean to . . . "

"It's OK. I understand how a woman out here all alone would have plenty of mistrust built up against strangers."

Clara nodded at the man and then looked out across the desert, "Thank you . . . ." She stopped in mid-sentence, her mouth frozen open.

McCaslin shot a look toward her, "What is it, Clara?"

She pointed to the northeast. Not more than three hundred yards out in the desert in the glare of the morning sun, a dark figure on horseback crested the top of a sand dune riding straight for the seep.

CHAPTER 18

The Sand Hills, Texas December 1868

"You smell that water?" Tig spoke in a cheerful tone to the mount beneath him. The brisk December morning had the horse feeling its oats. Feeling flush himself, with Jordie dead, he sank his spurs into the horse's flank. "Let's ride then."

The steed, not needing spurs for encouragement, picked up his legs and began a hard run over the top of a tall dune.

Tig knew this desert well. He had hidden here many times from a bothersome posse or sheriff. Most lawmen were reluctant to chase an outlaw across a desert teeming with blowing sand, rattlesnakes and Apaches. Up ahead, the green color of scrub trees appeared indicating water. With a little luck, he would pick up the woman's trail around the seep.

Tig reined the horse, slid out of the saddle and walked to the patch of scrub oak looking for any sign. To his left he noticed a set of hoof prints lightly indented in the sand and headed southwest away from the seep. *Fresh*, he thought. The flimsy wind blowing from the east had not yet covered them with sand. He stared with focused intent at the tracks and rubbed the back of his neck. Something didn't set right in his head. He kicked at the sand floor in frustration. *Way too clean.*

He studied the seep with a careful eye. In the back corner of the oak enclosure he spied where two branches had been broken from one of the trees. He moved closer and observed the green lying beneath the bark. He turned back and hurried out of the chaparral and into the desert. Grabbing his horse by the reins, he knelt and studied his own tracks. He glanced over to the tracks and let a wide smile carry across his face. Within seconds he had mounted his horse and spurred the animal hard toward the southwest.

"Looks like your plan worked." McCaslin glanced over to Clara.

"We'll see." Clara kept a watchful eye on the departing Tig Hardy.

"I thought you said there were two of them?" McCaslin inquired.

"There were." Clara frowned. "I think I know what that shot was this morning."

McCaslin stared at the dust following the rider. "Who is he, Clara?"

Clara rolled to her back and exhaled loudly, "I don't really know him. He rode onto our land four days ago in the middle of the night and burned our house and corral to the ground."

McCaslin threw an incredulous stare at Clara. "He burned you out?"

Clara rolled back over and scanned the horizon intently. "He beat my mother-in-law and kidnapped me. All I know is his name. He goes by Tig Hardy."

"Tig Hardy?" McCaslin gritted his teeth.

"Do you know him?" Clara bolted upright.

"No . . . No, I don't, but I know of him." McCaslin rose to his knees. "Some say he is the devil himself."

"I'm inclined to draw that conclusion as well." Clara spoke as Tig Hardy's dust disappeared under the horizon and from view. "Let's have some water and then I'll tend to your back." Her tone was weary. "Then we'll try and figure out our next move."

CHAPTER 19

The Sand Hills, Texas December 1868

The harshness of the desert sun burned red against Clara's closed eyes. She swallowed dryness and then licked her chapped lips. She slowly opened her eyes and glanced at McCaslin. His snoring caused the realization that they both had succumbed to fatigue earlier.

She rose, stretched and then dusted her shirt. The finely grained sand seemed to occupy more on the inside of her clothing than she did. A harsh wind had picked up from the north and tiny sand devils rose and spun skyward from the top of the surrounding dunes. Clara rubbed at her shoulders and looked to the northern skyline. A rich bank of purple clouds sat atop the horizon.

"Mr. McCaslin," she nudged the sleeping man, "Wake up, Mr. McCaslin."

"Huh?" he opened his eyes quickly.

"How do you feel?"

He opened his mouth several times and licked his lips. "I feel pretty good. What's going on?"

"I'm afraid we may have more trouble heading our way." Clara nodded northward.

McCaslin rose from the sand and stared at the northern sky. "That doesn't look like just a cold front to me."

Clara felt tears welling at her eyes. She clenched her jaw in an attempt to check her volatile emotions. "I was afraid you'd say that, Mr. McCaslin, I think we have a snow storm heading our way."

McCaslin turned his head to survey their surroundings. "There'll be a cold rain come first, Clara. We need to make shelter as best we can."

Clara nodded, fighting back her tears. "What do you suggest?"

"I think we best try to build a lean-to against the base of this dune. We're gonna need to get some scrub oak limbs to use as a frame." McCaslin rubbed his jaw and glanced to the seep below.

Clara stood and faced McCaslin. "Mr. McCaslin, I'm sorry I ran the horse off but I just didn't think the two of us stood a chance in trying to outrun Hardy."

McCaslin put a hand on Clara's shoulder. "Don't worry about that, Clara . . . ." He stopped mid-sentence and stared to the southwest.

"What is it?" She spun on her heels and stared across the desert.

"I can't be sure, but it sure looks like Hardy may have found your horse." He pointed at a spinning cloud of sand on the horizon.

Across the desert, they spotted a rider on a dead run for the seep with a horse in tow.

In the shadow of the towering sand dune, Clara curled up on her right side and listened with cautious intent for any sound from Hardy or his horse. An unrestrained nervousness rippled through her arms and shoulders, causing her upper body to twitch uncontrollably. Unable to stop the shivering, she pressed the Winchester deep into her body for support. McCaslin lay on his left side, his eyes in a fixed stare on her face.

"Ma'm." Hardy's voice broke the silence.

"I know you're up there, Ma'm."

Clara let a small whimper escape from her closed mouth. She looked to McCaslin who held his forefinger against his lips.

"Ma'm, please don't make me come up there after you." Hardy spoke with relative calm. "I've ridden a good ways to retrieve your horse, so there's no use in acting like you're not around."

McCaslin pointed to the rifle, asking in sign for Clara to pass it to him.

Tig pushed his hat back off his head and scratched his scalp. "It was your tracks, Ma'm. The imprints in the sand were very light as if the horse was riderless. That's what gave you away."

Clara shoved the rifle toward McCaslin and stifled a desire to cry aloud.

"I reckon the broken scrub branches were used to hide your footprints."

McCaslin eased a cartridge into the rifle chamber.

Angry at the silence, Tig yelled, "Ma'm, if I have to come up there, you won't like what I do next!"

"That won't be necessary." McCaslin rose from the cover of the sand hill and held the Winchester chest high on Hardy.

"Well lookey here." Tig laughed at the shirtless figure. "Robert Armstrong McCaslin. Present and accounted for, have you been watching over my hostage, McCaslin?"

Clara's eyes opened wide at the sound of McCaslin's name. With a sense of dread and disbelief, she rose and stared at the man next to her.

McCaslin hesitated, looked over at Clara and then slowly lowered the rifle. "Appears that way, Tig," he said.

Clara sat between her two captors with fists clenched, her back pinned against the scrub oak. The fear that consumed her minutes ago had been replaced by a sense of betrayal and anger. She stared into the distance but listened with a careful ear to the two men standing above her. She knew it was important to leave a sign for Free. It was imperative he know she was alive. And then she remembered the ripped sleeve stuffed into her pocket.

"Here you might want to put his on." Tig pulled a wool shirt from his saddle pack and tossed it toward McCaslin.

"You sure cut a wide path, Tig," McCaslin said as he pulled the shirt over his head with great care.

"I had business that needed tending to." Tig looked down at the woman and smiled. "Some of it is still unfinished."

"Well when this is over, I hope you plan to let Clara go." McCaslin tucked the shirt into his pants.

"You're not going soft on me are you, McCaslin?" Tig grinned.

McCaslin cleared his throat and looked at the larger man in front of him. "I don't care much for hurting a woman, that's all."

"Well, you let me decide about that and we'll stay the best of friends," Tig warned. "Now tell me how it is you came to be in the Sand Hills."

McCaslin scowled and then said, "We waited at the Pinery Station like you asked. We waited for a week past when you and Chase should have showed. At that point, the boys were restless and decided to ride out to Antelope Ridge and see if there were any drive cowboys making their way back to Texas. The Lowery brothers figured it would be easy pickings."

"How come you boys couldn't do what I told you?" Tig spat at McCaslin's feet. "It seems of late that cowboys who won't follow my orders end up dead."

"It seems following your orders gets a man the same result," McCaslin snapped back. He saw Tig's jaw tense and softened his voice. "It doesn't matter much now anyhow, Tig. The Apaches caught us below the hills and killed everyone."

"Everyone, but you," Tig stated and held McCaslin with a wide-eyed glance.

McCaslin gritted and then glanced back north. The once bright sky retreated south to escape the rippled waves of purple that rolled across the horizon like a thunderous herd of bison. "We've a storm coming, Tig, and if we want to hold up to the weather, we best go about making a shelter."

"No time for that. We're going to ride. I figure the woman's man is closing on us and I aim to meet him and his friend at the Pinery Station where we have an advantage."

Clara shot a questioning glance at the two men, "But there are only two horses."

Tig said flatly, "Don't worry none, Ma'm, you'll be riding with me."

"I'd rather she ride with me, Tig," McCaslin said as he adjusted the stirrups on Clara's horse.

Tig studied the man for a moment, tapped his pearl Colt handle and then bellowed in laughter. "OK, McCaslin, if that's what you want, lead the way out."

As the trio mounted up, Tig rode close to a scrub tree near the front edge of the seep. "Oh, and Ma'm, you forgot this." A ragged piece of shirt sleeve dangled between his fingers. "Your man will find out soon enough if you're dead or alive."

CHAPTER 20

The Sand Hills, Texas December 1868

A noticeable drop in temperature accompanied Free and Parks into the Sand Hills. The Kiowa dog ran far ahead of the horses with his nose near the ground. His back hair bristled in the sunlight at the warning smell of the man.

"How'd you come by the dog?" Parks asked.

"I found him with a Kiowa lance in his side the day Mother died."

"Well, he seems to have taken to you."

"I reckon it's more a partnership," Free said. "I figure the dog wants Hardy as bad as I do." Free pointed to the dog absorbed on the scent trail. "I think he knows Hardy's scent and is dead set on finding the man. I sure wouldn't want to be on the receiving end of his jaws. You should have seen what he did to a trader that tried to beef me at *Agua de Mesteño*."

"I met your trader friend," Parks smiled. "Last I saw of him, he was looking for his top-notch."

Free looked to his friend. "He was scalped?"

"I came upon him fighting with a band of Comanche. If I had known of your difficulty with him beforehand, I might have left him to the Indians. I also saw the two ruffians you left behind."

"Those two seemed well set on dying that day." Free cut off his words and focused on the dog.

At the base of a towering sand mound, the dog lifted his head into the wind and sniffed aggressively at the air. After processing the waves of scent, he dashed to the crest of the hill, barking at the air and kicking sand behind him. In seconds, he disappeared over the rise.

Free reined in Spirit, threw a glance to Parks and then tapped his spurs into Spirit's flank. He knew the loud cries that filled the air indicated the dog had found something.

A swarm of vultures darkened the sky as both men galloped to the base of the hill. Surprised by the scavengers, Free drew rein and gazed at the blackness. *Clara!* Fearing the worst, he slapped the reins hard across Spirit's neck and urged the horse up the shifting mountain of sand.

"Wait up, Free!" Parks shouted as the vultures circled above. "Don't go over the hill!" he warned in desperation.

"Com'on, Spirit!" Free gigged the Indian pony. "Git up, there!"

Frantic to beat Free over the hill, Parks spurred Horse forward and urged the pony to cross the dune first. The men reached the top together and crested the hill only to find the Kiowa dog eating on the hind quarter of a dead horse. A vile smell simmered in the air, causing both to cover their mouths and noses.

"Get away, Dog!" Free hollered as he rode close to the carcass. "Get outta there!"

The dog, claiming the animal as his own, looked back to Free with wildness in his eyes and bared his teeth.

"I wouldn't try to interrupt, Free!" Parks shouted. "He still has a lot of Indian in him!"

"What do you think this means?" Free asked as the dog flipped on his back and rolled in the carcass.

Parks surveyed the desert surface. "I don't know, but look at the tracks leading west. There were at least three horses riding in here."

Free leaned over Spirit's left shoulder and studied the

prints. "Let's see where they take us."

The men walked the mustangs along the desert floor. The godforsaken landscape presented a zigzagged trail of boot prints and horse tracks that melted together until no sense of direction could be determined. A few hundred yards from the dead horse a speck of darkness caught Free's eye. The unfocused blackness glistened brightly in the rippled air of the sand hills.

"Look there." Free pointed.

"I see it."

The men nudged their ponies toward the object. An anxious feeling of fear crept once more through Free's mind. He prayed that the darkness was simply a mirage, some kind of desert illusion and not his Clara. He had wished it so, just like his mother instructed. The tension strangled him and cut off his air, *Please*, he begged.

Against the whiteness of the desert, a lifeless body lay sprawled in the sand.

"Looks like Chase Hardy's friend," Parks said.

Free gulped air and stared at the corpse. A single gunshot wound dotted the man's forehead.

"Being a friend of Hardy doesn't seem to account for much," Parks shrugged.

"Why would Hardy shoot his accomplice?" Free asked.

Parks rubbed the back of his neck. "I don't know. You'd figure Hardy would want all the help he could muster. He has to know that both of us are tailing him. So it might be that this fella ran with Clara."

"Why would he risk that, knowing Hardy's reputation for being a hard case? He had to know Hardy would hunt him down and kill him."

"I don't know the whys. But look at it. Hardy rides into the trader's camp without Clara. Where would he have left her? This fella had to run off with her. Why else would Hardy take the desert route to the mountains?"

Free looked ahead and stared into the distant horizon. "So they're headed northwest?"

"That would take them straight into the Guadalupes," Parks said. He turned in his saddle to glance at the menacing sky behind them. "That wind is growing some teeth, Free. I don't like the feel of it." Parks sniffed the air. "Smells like rain and snow."

Free looked back, "More of that fuss, I suspect." He swung a leg over Spirit and jumped to the soft sand. He stood over the dead man and said, "We best get him in the ground before winter blows in on us."

Parks nodded and continued to search the sky, "After that we better look for shelter, a snow storm after a hard ride will break down these mustangs so they're unfit to run."

Free appraised the bleak desert surrounding them, "That might take considerable effort, Parks, cause all I see is sand and lots of it."

CHAPTER 21

The Guadalupe Mountains, Christmas Day 1868

At the approach to a mountain trail leading into the Guadalupes, Tig leaned from the saddle and snapped the branch of a live oak. Left to dangle in the wind, the limb would serve as a guidepost for anyone who followed the trio.

"You think that's wise, Tig?" McCaslin gazed at the broken branch as he rode past.

"McCaslin, you are really beginning to rile me. Why don't you let me worry about what's wise and what's not?" As Tig spoke, his gaze remained forward.

"All I'm saying, Tig, is you're not only leaving sign for the two following, but anyone one else in these mountains."

Tig reached up and snapped another limb as he rode by a line of trees. "I'll snap every limb on this mountain if I so choose, McCaslin! I'll also trample every blade of grass I see! I want those two cowboys coming straight up the trail to us!"

At five thousand feet and with snow falling, Tig sighted the limestone walls of the old Pinery Station. The white rock sat in marked contrast to the green of the surrounding high mountain pines.

The station offered a welcome invite to the road-weary trio. They rode through the lone entrance and pulled rein in the center of the enclosed pine stockade. Deserted for years, the old Pinery Station held favor with outlaws and renegades on the run from the law. The structure's walls stood eleven feet high, and the station contained its own water source. It was the perfect hideout.

"It ends here." Tig jumped from his horse and stretched his back. "Fetch the woman, McCaslin, and get her tied up. I don't need her running off now."

"Where's she gonna run to, Tig? We're five thousand feet into the mountains with wet snow falling. She'd die before she got a mile away."

Tig scowled at McCaslin's defiance and bit hard on his lip. "McCaslin! We're gonna need a fire to fight off this chill. I hope it's not too much trouble to ask her to do that!" he bellowed.

McCaslin dismounted and helped Clara from the horse.

"Get out of this cold, Clara," he said keeping a watchful eye on Hardy. "There's a fireplace inside, and I stocked in wood weeks ago."

"Why, Mr. McCaslin?" Clara asked. "You don't seem anything like him."

McCaslin gestured awkwardly toward the middle lean to. "Get inside before you catch the death, Clara. Take the bedroll with you."

"McCaslin!" Tig called. "We best get these horses in the corral and rubbed down."

McCaslin looked over to Tig and then glanced back to Clara, "I won't let anything happen to you, that I promise, Clara."

Inside the small, darkened, doorless room, Clara found a pile of kindling and a can of matches in the fireplace. She nested the kindling, placed a handful of shredded pine bark in the center and then held a lit match to the wood. Minutes later, warmth and smoke filled the double-sided fireplace. She knew it was urgent to get herself warm. She knew the baby would feel whatever she felt, and if she got sick so would the baby. She had to stay alive. *Alive and healthy.*

She removed the wet clothing that clung to her and hung them on a gun rack over the fireplace. Then she wrapped herself in the bedroll and began to rub her upper arms, trying to create much needed heat. "This is not how we were supposed to spend our first Christmas," she whispered to her child.

After a few minutes, the fire crackled and sparked as the dried pine logs were consumed in flames. Soon a spreading heat warmed her body and the room. She cradled her stomach and hummed softly, hoping the baby would recognize her voice.

"Clara, are you OK?"

Clara looked toward the doorway and saw McCaslin, "I'm fine, Mr. McCaslin."

"Who are you talking to?"

"It wasn't talk, I was humming a gospel song to my baby." Clara pulled the bedroll tighter around her shoulders.

McCaslin swallowed hard. "You're with child?"

"I am, sir." She returned her gaze to the flames dancing on the pine logs.

McCaslin walked into the dimly lit room and removed his hat. "Whatever you do, Clara, don't let Tig know that fact."

Clara turned her head and forced a tight smile. "What difference does it make, Mr. McCaslin? I'm sure he means to kill us all anyway."

"Don't say that, Clara. I told you I wouldn't let anything happen to you."

"Well, ain't this the sweetest thing." Tig stood in the station door, "I wonder what it was those Apaches did to your brain, McCaslin? Cause you seem to be all mush right now."

McCaslin spun and faced Hardy. "Maybe so, Tig. But I'm telling you right now; no harm comes to Clara."

Tig growled. "I'll tell you what, McCaslin. We'll sort that

out after her man and the cowboy are dead; 'til then you make sure you're up to the job ahead."

"Don't worry about me, Tig, I'll be up to it when the time presents itself."

Tig scratched his chin and stared at McCaslin, "I'm going out to pull the bars across the entrance gate. There's still a day's ration of beef in my saddle pack. You get that and the rest of the flour. I hate killing men on an empty stomach."

CHAPTER 22

The Old Pinery Station, Texas December 1868

The day after Christmas found the old Pinery Station covered in a light dusting of snow. Clara awoke to the charred smell of smoke as McCaslin and Hardy allowed the fire to burn out in the early morning hours.

Feeling the room's chill, she reached above the fireplace and removed her now dried clothing from the gun rack. She checked to make sure the men were still sleeping and then moved to a dark corner of the station room. With her back to the men, she wrapped the bedroll tightly around her body and put on her smoky, but fire-warmed woolen jeans and shirt.

"Don't worry about your privacy, Ma'm."

Clara swiveled at the voice.

"I'm not worried, Mr. Hardy."

"I have no yearning for colored or Indian women," Tig laughed.

Clara turned and held her head high, "I don't like you, Mr. Hardy. I've seen your kind all of my life. Men who hate for no other reason than the pleasure of it."

Tig clenched his jaw taut. "Watch your mouth, Ma'm, I'll not be spoken to that way by a woman, especially a colored woman."

Clara glared in defiance. "I pray that someday you can find a peace within yourself, Mr. Hardy."

Tig kept an angry stare on Clara, "That peace will be

coming soon, Ma'm, just as soon as your man arrives."

Clara stepped forward, "You might just find him more game than you wanted, Mr. Hardy. That is, if you don't aim to shoot him in the back."

"Why you little—" Tig raised his hand above his head. "I ought to—"

"What's going on here?" McCaslin rose from his bedroll and looked at Clara.

"Nothing, McCaslin." Tig snarled, "Why don't you get that fire breathing again and warm up this place?"

Clara held her ground and kept her gaze on Hardy.

"Clara?" McCaslin asked, "Everything OK?"

"Everything is fine, Mr. McCaslin," she looked to the fireplace.

"Let me help you with the fire."

Tig turned and stood in the open doorway of the room. "Yeah, you help *him* with the fire," he mocked.

McCaslin moved to the fireplace and began to blow on the darkened wood. In a matter of seconds a ribbon of orange embers began to glow on the remaining logs. "Man, some bacon and biscuits would taste good this morning." He rubbed his hands back and forth feeling the slow rising heat of the fire. "What do you think, Tig?" He looked toward the doorway.

Tig turned slowly toward the room and rubbed his tongue along his bottom lip.

McCaslin stared at the big man and wondered why he carried such a strange look on his face. "What is it, Tig? You look like you've set eyes on a ghost."

Tig staggered several steps into the room with both hands clutching his chest.

"Christ!" McCaslin yelled. Three arrows, all tipped with red hawk feathers, protruded from Tig's chest. "Clara! Get against the back wall!" he screamed. "Apaches!"

Tig fell forward with a loud smack on the dirt floor. His back held three more arrows.

McCaslin straightened and grabbed for the Winchester leaning against the fireplace. He quickly chambered a shell and moved to the right edge of the doorway. "Clara! Are you OK?" he called out.

"I'm fine!" Clara shouted back. "Do you see anything?" She scurried over and knelt behind McCaslin's back.

"Nothing," he whispered. "I warned him. He left sign all over the mountain." He grimaced at Hardy's lifeless body and then directed his attention to the gated entrance. "I sure wish we had a door. The station walls will protect us, but if those braves decide to rush all at once we'll both be up the flume."

A flash of color caught McCaslin's eye. Two braves crept forward in an attempt to remove the bars from the entrance gate. With the bars down, the band could easily ride into the stockade and rush the station room. McCaslin pulled the Winchester to his shoulder and sent two rounds into the nearest warrior. A spray of red colored the snow below the gate as the remaining Apache disappeared behind the pine stockade.

"I got one of them, but we're in for a bit of difficulty, Clara. I only have six rounds of ammunition on my belt and only three shells left in the rifle."

Clara looked over McCaslin's shoulder toward the entrance of the station. "What do we do?"

McCaslin turned to face her, "I don't know, but I need to get you away from here."

"What?" Clara questioned. "Where would I go?"

McCaslin swallowed hard. "Clara, there's something I wasn't straight with you or Tig about." He stared at Tig's body. "When we rode out with the Lowery brothers that day, Clem Lowery found an Apache squaw giving birth." He looked into Clara's eyes and shook his head. "You gotta believe me when I tell you the rest of us didn't have anything to do with it."

"With what, Mr. McCaslin? What happened?" Clara asked.

"Clem grabbed the squaw's baby and smashed its head on a rock." McCaslin leaned his head into the Winchester. "They raped the mother and then killed her." He sobbed. "That's why the Apaches chased us. They won't rest until all of us are dead. They want me, Clara! That's why you have to get out of here!" McCaslin stood and pulled Clara to her feet. "I owe you my life, and now I'm going to repay that. There's a small opening in the corral. You can sneak out the back way and ride east. If you go a mile or so from here, you'll pick up the old Mexican trail down the mountain. But you have to go now, Clara! Before they rush this place!"

"How can we risk moving to the corral?" Clara asked. "Listen to what you're saying."

McCaslin pointed to the fireplace. "I'll pull the wood out and you crawl through to the other side."

In the adjoining room, the doorway faced west and offered Clara full protection from the Apaches. As she crawled through the fireplace, a small piece of burnt wood caught her attention.

"Stay close to the wall, Clara," McCaslin hollered from the main room.

"When you reach the corral, don't waste time trying to saddle the horses, throw a blanket on one and lead the other on a stringer."

Clara looked back through the fireplace and stared incredulously at McCaslin,

"That leaves you afoot."

"When you get a hundred yards or so away from the station, cut the one horse loose and let him run. It might throw the Apaches off your trail! If you can make it 'til nightfall, you should be safe. The Apache don't like to fight or trail after dark!"

"Mr. McCaslin!" Clara shouted, "How are you going to get out of here?"

"Ride and don't stop, Clara. No matter what you hear or

how safe you think it is, keep riding. Ride until you find people."

"I can't just leave you, Mr. McCaslin." A solitary tear ran from Clara's eye.

"Go now!" McCaslin said wide eyed. "Go now, Clara! Save your baby before it's too late!"

CHAPTER 22

The Guadalupe Mountains, Texas
December 1868

After a punishing night of freezing temperatures and snow at the Apache Seep, Free and Parks rose in the early morning hours and rode the hundred miles to the *Ojo Aridó* trail located two thousand feet below the Old Pinery Station. The Kiowa dog appeared every now and then, running ahead of the horses in the prairie grass with his nose pushed low to the ground.

The two fatigued men began the grueling climb up the balance of the trailhead late in the afternoon. The temperature was well above freezing, but with a cloudless night looming, the prospect of another miserable evening stirred in both men's minds.

At one thousand feet up Free noticed a trail no wider than a man's boot cutting into the *Ojo Aridó*. "Look at this, Parks." He motioned toward the ground.

"Appears to be moccasin tracks," Parks said, surveying the trail. "I'd say a band of fifteen or more cut across here and headed up the mountain." He stared up toward the station.

"Kiowa?" Free asked.

"I reckon them to be Apache." Parks opened the tobacco pouch hanging from his neck and removed a plug. "But I can't figure why they would be this far to the east during winter."

Free lifted the tobacco pouch from inside his shirt and opened the neck. The leather pouch carried his thoughts back to the morning when Clara presented the gift to him. What seemed like a lifetime ago had in reality happened only seven days earlier. He smiled as he remembered that morning in the kitchen with his mother. He cast a blank gaze up the trail and became lost in his thoughts. He wondered if he would find Clara waiting for him at the station. He wondered if he would be able to hold her again. And he wondered if he would have the opportunity to kill Tig Hardy. For as sure as he breathed, he knew an ambush awaited them.

"Free? You OK?"

Jarred back to the present, Free turned toward his friend and regrouped his thoughts. "I'm fine, Parks." He glanced back down at the tracks. "Why do you think it's Apache? I thought they had all retired to the reservation."

"Most have," Parks said, "but there are a few bands left hiding in the mountains, causing a whole lot of trouble for the U.S. and Mexico."

"Looks like one stayed here with the horses while the others climbed the mountain," Free said, and then pushed a cut of tobacco deep into his jaw.

"I reckon the main bunch headed up to the station." Parks stared across the trail, "But look over there." He pointed to a spot where the Kiowa dog was busy taking in the numerous forest smells, "The dog has picked up something. I'll bet the brave guarding the horses moved the herd across the trail and walked them back to the east." He pulled his Winchester from its leather scabbard. "We might have more than just Tig Hardy to deal with at the end of this climb." He chambered a shell into the rifle and set the rifle butt against his saddle.

Free pulled the Sharps from his ring and held the rifle across his chest. "Guess we best get up this trail then and see what kind of party is waiting on us."

"More of your fuss, I suspect." Parks lightly tapped Horse

with a spur and walked the mustang forward.

"One thing bothers me though, Parks."

"What's that?"

"It seems mighty quiet on this mountain right now."

Parks turned an ear up the hill and listened for several seconds, "You're right, Free, way too quiet," he said.

CHAPTER 23

The Old Pinery Station, Texas December 1868

The old Pinery Station showed no signs of life. The wooden bars used to barricade the entrance lay scattered near the gate and a trail of blood stained the snow. An eerie quiet surrounded the stockade, giving Free and Parks pause.

Both men sat in a clump of pines a hundred feet from the fortress, trying to take measure of their situation.

Free surveyed the entire compound and saw no movement or sign of life. A nagging fear tugged at his heart that told him he would not find Clara here.

"Will that dog listen to you?" Parks asked.

"I don't know." Free glanced at the animal several yards away. The dog sat on his haunches with his ears erect.

"See if you can persuade him to move inside the gate. If anyone is in the station, he'll let us know." Parks kept his gaze on the station walls.

"Dog." Free pointed toward the station, "Go on, dog. Get in there."

The animal turned his head toward Free, stood, and stared at the entrance.

"Go on now!"

Obeying the command, the dog exploded forward and sprinted to the station. The dog stopped at the gate and sniffed each wooden bar; he then began to lick the ground just inside the entrance.

"What is it, boy?" Free called out.

The dog turned back to Free, sniffed the air, and then ran inside the stockade. After several seconds of quiet, the dog began to bark. Soon, the barking became louder and incessant.

"He's found something!" Free looked over to Parks.

"Let's go!" Parks slapped the reins across Horse's shoulders.

Inside the stockade, a scalped corpse lay face-up in the snow several feet from the middle station room. Parks jumped from Horse and inspected the arrow-riddled body.

"It's Hardy. Captain Huntt was right, he and Chase looked exactly alike," he said. "And these arrows are all flecked with hawk feathers. I reckon we're dealing with Apaches for sure."

Directed by the dog's yips and howls, Free dismounted, maneuvered around Hardy's lifeless body and staggered into the station's main room. "Clara!" he cried out. His chest pounded explosively with the fear of what he might find. Three feet from the fireplace, a man lay belly down with his hands and feet staked to the earthen floor. A long, length of leather strap encircled the man's forehead. Tied to a peg between his legs, the strap pulled the man's head back and forced him to stare into a still burning fire.

"Parks!" Free screamed.

Parks ran into the room and grimaced at the sight before him. "Christ!" He turned back toward the door, "They roasted him alive." Taking a deep breath, he turned back to the room and drew his knife. He cut the leather strap and allowed the man's head to fall to the floor. "I don't know who this man was, Free, but the Apaches don't kill like this unless something horrible was done to one of their own."

Free looked away and gasped for breath. "I don't know what a man could do to warrant that kind of death."

Parks looked at the man's hands. He had scraped the flesh from his fingers digging in the dirt from the pain. "Let's get him and Hardy covered before I get sick," he said.

"What about Clara?" Free cried out in anguish, "Where could she be?"

Parks looked up. "There are two station rooms adjoining this one. You search the east room, and I'll search the west."

Free nodded and ran hurriedly toward the doorway, calling in desperation, "Clara! Clara!"

"Free!" Parks called to his friend's back, "Don't go in that room without your Colt drawn!"

Parks moved into the west room heedful of what he might find inside. The main body of the area was coated gray by shadows of the approaching evening. Even in the near darkness, Parks could see the room was empty. Dejected that Clara was not here, he turned to exit the shadiness. From the open doorway, the remaining daylight illuminated a small section of the back wall. There, scribbled in charcoal was a written message.

"Free," he shouted in excitement, "Get over here, quick!"

Free pressed both hands against the station room wall and gently patted the cool limestone. Head down, he exhaled fully and uttered, "She's alive." He lifted his gaze and stared once more at the words written in charcoal.

December 26 Morning

Free, I am alone and on horseback.

I am riding east to the Old Mexican Trail.

Hurry.

Clara.

Parks placed a hand on his friend's shoulder. "We best ride, Free. Clara's got a five-or-six hour head start on us, but if we use the dog, we might find her before dark."

"How is he going to pick up her scent, Parks?"

Parks studied his friend in a measured gaze and then stared at the leather string around his neck, "Let him have a smell of your tobacco pouch. Her scent should be all over it."

As night descended through the forest pines, a noticeable chill settled toward the ground. Clara looked around the graying woods and shivered uncontrollably. She was exhausted but felt fortunate to be alive. Mr. McCaslin's rifle had gone silent only minutes after she fled the station. At first she figured the Apache would track her down in short order. But true to his word, Mr. McCaslin had saved her life, for the Apaches spent several hours torturing and tormenting him. His screams had filled the mountain and followed her for an eternity. His death was a grim reminder of how fragile life was for those who chose to settle in the West.

She looked up at the clear winter sky. She knew that meant another night of freezing temperatures. She considered building a small fire, but realized even a small flame might signal her location.

She had zigzagged across the Mexican trail on her descent, praying the north to south pattern would confuse any trackers. The process had been slow and tiring, but if McCaslin was correct, she would be safe from the Apache during the night. And with any luck at all, she would wake with tomorrow's sunrise to a dazzling view of the prairie desert below the Guadalupes.

"Whoa, horse." She pulled back on the reins. "We'll take our rest here tonight."

The darkness spread faster now and Clara hurried to secure the horse to a pine. Weary and lonely, she placed her back against the tree and pulled the saddle blanket over her shoulders for warmth. "I'll get you some browse tomorrow, I promise," she spoke to the horse.

The horse moved nervously on its hind legs at her words and seemed skittish. Exhausted, Clara squinted into the charcoal forest with a fixed stare. It looked as if the trees were moving. *Get a hold of yourself, Clara*, she thought. *You've come too far to go crazy now*. Smiling at the notion of trees moving, her eyes drooped slightly and as sleep approached, a series of light kicks tapped on the bottom of her boots. With eyes closed, a smile quickly spread across her mouth. "Free?" She lifted her eyes sleepily, "I knew you'd find me . . . ." She stopped mid-sentence, shocked by the Apache looming over her.

The Apache grabbed Clara's wrists and with little exertion yanked her to her feet.

Caught off guard, she stared with wide eyes at the formidable warrior and uttered, "Who are . . ." but before she could finish her sentence, the Apache brave swung her around so her back was to the trail. From behind, a rawhide strap fell across her face and into her open mouth. She struggled against the Apache's grip and shook her head frantically as the tightened strap pulled her mouth into a distorted smile. A rush of energy surged through her body, she tried to scream, but only a muffled utterance issued from the Apache gag.

CHAPTER 24

Near El Paso del Rio del Norte, Mexico
December 1868

After a day's ride out of the Guadalupes, the Apache raiding party crossed the great north river at a spot several miles south of El Paso del Rio del Norte. Clara shared a horse with a young brave the others called Delshay. Delshay had pulled her hands forward under his arms and then tied her wrists at his waist, forcing her tight against his back. The rawhide gag bit deeply into the corners of her mouth and trickles of blood oozed from the binding.

Exhausted, hungry and stiff-backed, Clara, nevertheless, pushed all her pain aside. The Apache never spoke and seemed to suffer little effect from the cold and the continuous riding. *Act like an Apache, Clara,* she told herself. It might be the only way to guarantee both her and the baby's safety. *Free and Parks must be following close*, she thought. She had heard their far away calls echoing throughout the mountains during the previous night. *Concentrate, Clara!* she demanded. *Do whatever is necessary until Free comes!*

In the last hour of darkness, the Apache band came to rest in a small mesquite thicket. The group's leader, a warrior called Chan-deisi, signaled for the warriors to dismount. Delshay untied her wrists, swung his right leg over the horse's head and jumped to the ground. He looked up at Clara and held one finger to his lips. Clara nodded at his warning, and then the brave pulled her off the horse.

Clara rubbed each wrist gingerly, relieved to be on her feet and free of the rawhide binding. Delshay drew his knife and held the flint blade very close to her eyes. His expression, cold as the north wind, admonished her to stay quiet. He moved the blade to the side of her head and with a deft stroke cut her gag. Clara pulled the embedded leather strap from her mouth and hurled it to the ground. Delshay laughed at her action and removed a small calf bladder from around his hip. He untied the drawstring and pushed the bladder toward her.

Clara greedily grabbed for the water and drank. After only a few swallows, Delshay pulled the bladder from her grasp and returned it to his waist. Clara wiped her mouth with the back of her hand and winced as the brine water stung her cut lips. Delshay once again held a finger to his lips and then pressed on her shoulders, forcing her to sit.

On the ground, Clara arched her back and rubbed her stomach with a gentle touch. The circular motion of her hands calmed her thoughts, which she hoped relaxed the baby.

The rest of the band milled about, gathering dead mesquite sticks and picking any remaining beans from the trees. Clara's stomach growled noisily from lack of food, and she prayed the rumblings would not alarm the Apache braves.

One of the older braves removed a fire drill and kindling pouch from his quiver. The others crowded at the brave's back and appeared excited as the fire-maker rolled the drill back and forth in a pinch of sand. Shortly, a spark began to smoke in the drill base and the brave fanned the smoke with the kindling pouch. As the kindling began to flame, he carefully added larger and larger mesquite twigs to his creation.

Walking from the group, Delshay approached Clara and smiled broadly. He opened his right hand and exposed several dried pods of mesquite beans. He pointed to his mouth repeatedly with the other hand. Starving, Clara grabbed the pods and began shelling the beans. She hungrily ate the bitter-tasting beans, thankful for the nourishment. Delshay nodded at her appetite and then motioned for her to follow him back to the fire.

Kneeling beside the fire, one of the braves carefully unrolled a small square of deerskin. A second brave stood nearby and held a short length of mesquite branch sharpened on one end. The first brave lifted a blond scalp from the deerskin and poked it onto the limb. Horrified, Clara stiffened at the sight and felt the burning sensation of bile rise in her throat.

The Apache began to chatter excitedly as the first brave then lifted a dark-haired scalp and pushed it onto the pointed stick. The second brave turned and held the impaled scalps over the small fire. In seconds, the smell of burning flesh filled the air and crept into Clara's nose. She looked away and jerked spastically with dry heaves.

Delshay spun around and issued a stern look of disgust by her interruption. "*Gunjule!*" he warned her to behave. And then he held a finger to his lips. The rest of the raiding party stopped and stared at her with twisted expressions. "*Gunjule!*" Delshay repeated his warning once more.

Clara nodded and regained her composure. "I'm sorry." She lowered her head in respect and hoped she had not angered the raiding party. After a moment of silence, Delshay looked back to the group, and the chatter resumed. Her indiscretion apparently forgiven, Clara exhaled softly, caressed her stomach and reminded herself to remain strong.

After removing the scalps from the fire, the two braves worked with attentive care on their trophies. Each softened the burnt side by pounding the scalp with a small stone. Next, each brave scraped the remaining flesh away with the cutting edge of his knife. Clara watched, both disgusted and intrigued at the Apache's workmanship. With the process of cleaning and softening finished, they tied the scalps to a mesquite hoop, using strands of horsehair. As the sun gradually climbed over the horizon, the two braves lifted their coup skyward, offered thanks to the Sun God, and asked for his protection.

With the morning properly welcomed, the braves kicked sand on the remaining flames and extinguished the fire. Three Apache braves peered from the scrub and studied the settlement a few hundred yards to the north. The scattering of houses was located a mile south of the more populated El Paso del Norte. The trio hunkered low to the ground and exited the mesquite stand intent on reaching the first line of outbuildings undetected.

As soon as the braves departed, the remaining warriors took to their ponies ready to ride or fight. From his mustang, Delshay held an outstretched arm toward Clara. With great reluctance, she grabbed the extended hand and pulled herself up. Delshay pulled her arms through to his stomach and once again tied her wrists securely.

In the settlement, the Mexican inhabitants emerged from their homes to begin their daily chores. Soon, a great number of workers occupied the fields on the eastern side of the settlement. Some of the laborers dug sotol bulbs while others moved toward the river to collect water. In the midst of this activity, the three Apache moved inconspicuously into the yard of the nearest home. It was as if they were invisible.

Cautious in their movements, the trio circled the house and remained out of sight for several minutes. They reappeared on a dead run, racing for the clump of mesquites. Two of the braves carried large objects slung over their shoulders while the third brave kept a watchful eye on the Mexican workers.

The braves returned to the scrub undetected. The rest of the raiding party welcomed their success with a great slapping of thighs. The two braves showed wide smiles as they tossed the plunder across their pony's shoulders.

Even with her view partially blocked, Clara nonetheless could see the swag was Mexican children. The gagged children kicked hopelessly at the air and a terrified look of helplessness glowed in their eyes. Clara tried to make eye contact with each, but the chaos of the moment made it impossible. She started to call out and then thought better of her foolishness. All she could do now was wait and bide her time.

With everyone mounted, Chan-deisi whirled his horse to the south and kicked the pony's flank. "*Nzhoo*!" He shouted to show his approval of their raid. "*Nzhoo*!" The rest of the band hollered back. And then in a swirl of dust, the raiding party raced from the scrub thicket and disappeared into the Mexican desert.

CHAPTER 25

The Guadalupe Mountains, Texas
December 1868

In the shade that follows day and later turns to night, Free rubbed his hand in a patch of scuffed-up ground near the Old Mexican Trail. He felt certain that Clara had been here. "Looks like the same pony tracks we found below the Old Pinery Station."

"Makes sense," Parks answered from across the trail, "And what do you make of this?" He held up a saddle blanket abandoned near a towering pine.

Free walked over and stared carefully at the blanket. "Hard to say." He looked back and pointed to the tracks. "There's prints over there for fifteen horses, and then they just vanish from the mountain."

The Kiowa dog ran to the blanket with his nose held high in the air. He sniffed every inch of the fabric and then began to jump and claw at one corner.

"What is it, boy?" Free asked, concerned.

The dog lifted his head and sniffed into the blackness. Aroused by a scent, he issued an angry, rolling growl directed up the mountain trail.

Parks gazed into the distance toward the higher peaks of the Guadalupe range. "The dog seems all fired up that the trail leads north."

Free scanned the mountain above and shouted in frustration, "Clarrrahh!" He waited several seconds as the echo circled the hillside, and then he called again, "Clarrrahh!" He fixed his gaze on the black peaks above. "Why would they travel to higher ground in the dark and cold?"

Parks shook his head, confused by the dog's signal. "I don't know. You'd reckon they'd follow the trail down the mountain and into the scrub prairie." He glanced at Free, "What do you want to do?"

Free slipped the reins over Spirit's head and stepped up in the stirrup. "I guess we ride up the mountain."

Under the soft light of the moon, Free and Parks followed the Kiowa dog up the rock-strewn mountainside. The treacherous terrain forced the men to walk their mustangs tardily as a misstep on the scattered chunks of limestone could easily snap a cannon bone.

"Free, I know you don't want to hear this, but we've got to stop," Parks said. "These ponies need water and rest. We've been riding the trail for almost a full day."

Free nodded his understanding. "I know, Parks, but we're bound to be close. What if we stop now and Clara's only a little ways off? I couldn't live with that."

Parks rode close to his friend. "We'll be no good to Clara if we don't get some rest, Free. Fighting while you're tired is foolish. Fighting Apache while you're tired is a death request. Let's give these ponies a rub and take a few hours of rest. By that time, the sun should be on the rise and we can follow the Apache trail in the daylight."

Free reluctantly pulled on Spirit's rein and patted the mustang's neck. "You're right, Parks. I know you are. And I know better than to go off in the dark like this, but the thought of Clara out there with the Apache is twisting my gut into knots."

Parks nodded helplessly, “We’ll find her, Free. I promise we’ll find her.”

The men dismounted and unsaddled the mustangs. After wiping down each with a wool rag, they allowed the horses to graze unfettered on the mountainside.

“We best not risk a fire.” Parks pulled the last of their jerked beef from his saddle pack.

Free nodded and removed the water bladder from around his saddle. “I’m getting accustomed to these dry camps anyhow,” he said.

After a small portion of meat and water, Free lay back against his saddle and under the shadow of Guadalupe Peak wondered what sunrise would bring.

The December sun rose in a fiery ball of red. Great streaks of daybreak raced from the horizon and chased the morning chill westward. Free woke to loud barking. The Kiowa dog raced from up the mountainside and into camp growling and yipping with puppy-like exuberance.

“What’s he so happy about?” Parks woke and leered at the dog from beneath the brim of his hat.

“I think he wants us up.”

The dog ran full bore to Free’s side, licked his face several times, and then ran toward the mustangs.

“Dog!” Free admonished the animal with a stern voice. “Quit it!”

Unheeding, the dog ran circles around the ponies and then raced up the trailhead. Several yards up the trail, he turned, barked loudly at both men and then rushed toward the peak.

“I guess we best get up; he’s not likely to let us rest any longer.” Free stood, looked at the morning sun and then arched his back. “Man, am I feeling old.”

Parks leaned forward from his saddle and rocked his neck back and forth. “We’re getting soft, Free. Too much sleeping on feather mattresses lately, I reckon."

Free pulled his saddle from the ground and walked toward Spirit, "It doesn't take long to get used to the comforts of life, that's for sure."

The men rode up the mountain trail toward Guadalupe Peak. The dog's interminable barking served as both roadmap and aggravation to the two.

"What do you think he's got now?" Parks asked.

"I don't know. But that constant yapping would make a preacher take up cussing."

Parks looked over to his friend. "Well, his barking doesn't carry the concern as before. You figure if he had found the Apache band, there would be a whole lot of growling coming out of him."

At the crest of the next rise, the dog came into view. He charged full bore at a dead horse sprawled on a mound of limestone. Two arrows protruded from the mustang's neck. In almost play-like fashion, the dog emitted a low rumbling sound at the dead beast and barred his teeth to show his displeasure. Free and Parks rode close to the dog and dismounted.

Free stared at the dead animal and then turned back to Parks. "What does this mean?"

Parks pushed his hat back and exhaled slowly.

"What is it, Parks?"

"It means there's an Apache brave buried under that horse."

"That's *why* they traveled up the mountain?"

"This is a sacred place. I reckon they figured it best to bury him here. But this dead Apache may present a mess of difficulty in getting Clara back."

"What?" Free jerked his head toward Parks. "What do you mean?"

"I mean that band can't return to the village victorious now. And those scalps they took are now worthless."

Free shrugged. “I still don’t understand what that has to do with getting Clara back?”

Parks pulled his hat back down and bit on his lower lip. “These braves have to capture as many hostages as possible on their way back to the winter camp. It’s the only way they can make amends for losing a warrior.”

Free grimaced, “And they aim to keep all their hostages as Apache?”

“The dead brave’s mother will demand a new son from the leader of this raid and the rest of the hostages will be kept as slaves or sold to border traders.”

Free dropped to one knee and removed his hat. “Like those two at *Agua de Mesteño*?” He rubbed his brow.

“The very same. Polk told me those two were Comanchero, but I’ll bet they traded with all the tribes.” Parks turned and looked west. “I figure the band that has Clara must winter to the south near the Rio Grande. That country is full of broken mountain range.”

Free gazed out toward Mexico, “What do we need to do to get Clara back? She’s carrying a child, Parks and who knows what hardships she’ll endure in an Apache winter camp.”

Parks placed a hand on his friend’s shoulder and squeezed gently. “You’re going to have to trust me, Free.”

Free looked up, “You know I’ll always do that. What do we need to do?” He repeated, anguished.

“First, we need to drop this trail and ride down to the prairie. Next, we need to round-up a Mesteño herd as quickly as possible.”

“Wild mustangs?” Free asked, concerned. “Why?”

“We’re going to do some bartering with our Apache friends, but if we aim to keep our scalps we best not ride into their camp empty-handed.”

CHAPTER 26

The Apache Winter Camp, Texas
January 1869

Near a long, sweeping bend of the Rio Bravo, the Apache raiders crossed back into Texas. Clara, asleep against Delshay's back, was startled awake by a great splashing of water and the thunderous clatter of hooves on river rock. She had endured eight long days tied to Delshay as the raiding party navigated the torturous Mexican desert. From her short time with the Apache, Clara had come to realize that they could survive in a land where most other men would perish.

Ahead of her, the captured children, slung over their captors' ponies like killed deer, lifted their heads as high as possible to avoid drowning. The Apache had raided several villages en route to the winter campground and the captured children now numbered seven, two boys and five girls. The Apache hobbled the children at night, and the only food given them during the long journey was the stomach milk of a rustled calf. Clara noticed that the seven children were very young, not one appeared to be over the age of eight. She figured the Apache knew that young children adapted easier to a captive's life. A small tear dotted the corner of her eye as she tried to imagine what fate lay ahead for her, her child, and the seven captured children.

The Apache, vigorously pursued by Mexican bounty hunters and the feared Tejanos, hid their winter camp in an offshoot canyon deep inside Cañon de Sierra Carmel. Sheer limestone walls protected the village on three sides, and lookouts posted along the cliffs could scan the mountainous landscape for miles in all directions. By the time Chan-deisi and his warriors forded the shallow waters of the great river, all of the Apache camp, alerted to their return, waited for the whoops and cries that signaled a successful raiding party.

Clara peered over Delshay's shoulder at the spectacle of the Apache winter camp. Fifty tepees were scattered against the back of the canyon with all of their openings facing southeast. Racks of thinly sliced meat dried in the warm January sun and several clay pots cooked in a communal fire pit.

As was the custom when a warrior died in battle, the raiding party approached in solemn quiet. Several of the squaws who recognized the meaning of the silence, broke from the assembled band and ran toward Chan-deisi. The squaws beat their breasts and shouted loudly at the sky. Clara wrapped her hands tighter around Delshay, alarmed at the reception. The angry mob circled them, and began to pull the now terror-stricken children from the mustangs.

The oldest of the squaws ran to the left side of Chan-deisi's mustang. She pounded her fists on Chan-deisi's leggings and cursed him in an ear-splitting wail. Chan-deisi dismounted and tossed his right hand skyward. He walked toward the men of the band, all the while suffering the abuse and curses from the old squaw.

At Chan-deisi's signal, Delshay cut Clara's bindings and then leapt from his pony. He looked up at her and held his finger to his lips, "*Gunjule*," he said and then trudged solemnly through the howls of the Apache women. He stopped one of the women who held her head bowed to her chest and pointed in great animation toward his pony. The woman nodded, moved past the other squaws and approached the mustang.

Clara, free of Delshay, sat motionless, unsure of what to do next. She rubbed her wrists and watched as Chan-deisi and Delshay moved past the squaws and then disappeared into a large tepee decorated with many bison hides.

"You come down."

Clara glanced down at a young squaw. "You speak English?" she asked, amazed.

The squaw grabbed Clara's wrist and yanked her from the pony to the ground, "You do as I say. You will be OK." She nodded toward the squaws, "They only take the children."

Clara rose and stared intently at the figure before her. Even with a sun-bronzed face, this most certainly was a white woman.

"Who are you?"

"Follow," the young squaw lowered her head once more and ushered Clara away from the building chaos; "the children will be OK."

Clara turned back and looked on horrified. The older squaws held each child by the ear, dragging them toward a gauntlet of young squaws and Apache children. "What are they doing!" she cried.

"Shhh." The white squaw cautioned. "*Gode*."

"I don't understand," Clara said, frantic.

The white squaw grabbed Clara's hand and led her to a tepee near the creek. "The dream spirit," she replied, "A brave from the raiding party has been killed. The dream spirit lives in the bodies of children. The *gode* must be driven from the children so the camp will not be cursed."

"But, that's crazy!" Clara objected.

"Not crazy. It is our way. The children will be good." The squaw looked about and then quickly pushed Clara into the tepee.

Clara knelt on one of several bison hides that covered the floor.

"I am called Dayden," the white squaw said, "Delshay's wife."

"You're white."

"I *was* white. A long time ago, before the Apache. But no one from my people came to claim me. So now I am Apache."

Clara leaned forward and grasped Dayden's hand, "Can you help me?" she asked.

Dayden patted Clara's hand gently, "I can help you to live but not to escape."

"I have a child inside," Clara said, desperate.

"I know," Dayden smiled, "Delshay spoke of this. He is wise and knows such things. He wishes it a boy."

Clara leaned back, confused. "He wishes?"

"Yes, you are very strong, for Delshay to take you as a wife."

"His wife?" The words whirled through Clara's head. "His wife," she stated, wearily. A sudden heaviness descended on her shoulders and a rush of emotion forced her to sob uncontrollably.

Dayden held Clara's shoulders and softly rocked her back and forth. "It is the baby," she whispered in Clara's ear; "he is happy and sends you tears as his sign."

Clara hugged Dayden and exhaled softly, "Yes, it is the baby's sign." She wiped her eyes and steeled her mind for what might follow. If Delshay thought she was strong, she must stay strong. Averse as the thought was of becoming an Apache wife, she realized it might be the only way to protect her and the baby until Free came for them. "And the children?" she pointed outside the tepee flap, "what about them?"

Dayden smiled, "The children will be good."

Clara smiled but turned away from the flap, unable to listen to the cries of the seven captured children.

CHAPTER 27

The Comancheria, Texas January 1869

Free, Parks and the Kiowa dog lay on their stomachs behind the cover of a three-foot dirt mound adorned in yucca. The prairie hump was the highest point for miles on the flat land of the southwestern Comancheria. Parks trained field glasses on a herd of twenty mustangs that grazed two hundred yards upwind. The herd browsed in a tight circle eating on dried prairie grasses and mesquite brush.

"*Mesteño*," Parks grinned, "that browse would kill a cavalry horse."

"How many do you figure we need to capture in order to barter with the Apache?" Free asked, anxiously. They had trailed this herd for over a week since leaving the Guadalupes, and he was frantic with concern about Clara.

"I reckon we best take them all." Parks rolled over on his back and lifted the tobacco pouch from beneath his shirt. "We can't afford to ride into an Apache camp and be short. We're going to need every one of those ponies."

Free glanced at the grazing herd and then looked at Parks. "That might take weeks."

"More likely, a month." Parks pushed the chaw into his jaw, "In this country, it will take some doing just to get close to them."

Free returned his gaze to the prairie and then rolled over

on his back. "It's flat for a long ways, that's for sure."

Parks stared up at the cloudless sky quiet and lost in his thoughts. "We've got the two fastest ponies on the prairie, Free. I know we could swoop down on that herd and rope a couple of mares, but the others would scatter, and we'd waste another two weeks trying to get them back together."

Free reached inside his shirt and removed his tobacco pouch. "Are you certain this is the best way to get Clara back?" he asked.

Parks twisted to his side and looked at Free. "Afraid so. The Apache take captives for only two reasons; one is to replace a lost tribe member and the other is for trade. If we hold good mustangs, like those out there, we ought to be able to trade for Clara."

Free dipped into the pouch and pulled out a plug of tobacco. "We best work out a plan then, because I can't bear to have Clara a captive any longer than need be."

Parks sat up and took a long hard look at the mustang herd. He untied the bandana from around his neck, mopped at his forehead, and then announced, "What we need is a Judas goat."

"A what?"

"You know, a goat used to lead the rest of the herd to slaughter."

Free winced, "Those aren't goats out there."

"No, but a mustang follows a herd just the same."

"And where would you propose we find a Judas goat in the middle of the Comanche prairie?"

Parks gazed over at Horse and chewed at his lip, "You're looking at him," he grinned.

"Horse?"

Parks got to his feet and strolled over to the mustang. He uncinched the girth belt and removed the saddle from Horse's back. "I'm going to let Horse see if he can get close to the lead mare."

Free pushed his hat back and scratched his head. "You're going to do what?" he asked, confused.

Parks gently rubbed the inside of Horse's left ear. The mustang relaxed his body and stood perfectly still, thoroughly enjoying the massage. "Most folks think the dominant stallion leads a wild herd, but it's not always that way. Look down at that bunch. The dominant male is on the outside of the herd circle."

"Isn't that where he needs to be to defend his herd?"

Parks removed his finger and patted Horse's neck, "Yes, but that doesn't give him dominance. The herd leader is inside the circle. Males and low positioned females stay on the herd's edge. If there's trouble, they get to face it first." Parks stroked the bridge of Horse's nose. "We're going to see if Horse can entice that dominant female to run with him."

Free stared at Horse. "But that means he's going to have to fight and defeat the dominant stallion."

"Unless you have a better idea, that's all I can come up with." Parks leaned over and whispered in Horse's ear for several minutes.

When Parks had finished, Horse bounced his head up and down several times and then trotted onto the prairie toward the wild mustangs.

Even upwind, the dominant stallion, a short brutish buckskin, seemed to sense the intruder. The nervously agitated stallion snorted and lifted his nose high into the wind to survey the surrounding prairie. When he spotted Horse's approach, he squealed several times to announce his territory boundary.

Horse, undeterred by the stallion's show, continued toward the mares at a steady gait. The anxious stallion, uneasy at an intruder's presence, lowered his head and began pawing clumps of prairie dirt over his back. Not to be outdone, Horse snorted back at the buckskin and bounced his head from side to side. The stallion, clearly riled by the upstart's refusal to stop, extended his neck forward, pulled his upper lip back and screamed loudly.

Horse understood the stallion's message of *stay away*, but he raced forward with his head held erect. Several yards from the stallion, he stopped short and sent a spray of prairie dust at his opponent. Horse stomped at the ground, and then proceeded to stand nose to nose with the stallion. He pulled his ears back and opened his mouth wide to display his own aggression.

The stallion, vexed by the interloper, tossed his head from side to side, snorted, pawed the ground, and pushed against Horse's head. Horse refused to be intimidated and arched his head as high as possible in an attempt to look larger than the stallion.

After several minutes of smelling the air, the stallion turned and kicked angrily at Horse. Horse instinctively dodged the thrust, circled and then landed a well-placed kick to the stallion's side. Caught off guard, the stallion stumbled forward and toppled to his knees. As he struggled to regain his legs, Horse whirled and bit deeply into the stallion's cheek. Blood rushed from the bite and streamed down the stallion's jaw. The vicious bite exposed nerve endings to the air and caused the stallion to falter in his attempt to stand. Horse recognized the hesitation and burst forward, butting his foe to the ground.

Caught by surprise at his rival's strength, the stallion rolled awkwardly onto his back and thrashed at the air with flailing legs. In unbridled fury, he turned his head to the left, rolled back to his feet and blew hot steam from his nostrils. Upright, he regained his composure and exploded toward Horse.

Horse met the charge head-on in a fit of rage. Both animals reared, biting and screaming at each other. The grace of their movements belied the viciousness of their head-to-head battle. Horse lunged at the stallion's head with his front legs and then fell back on all fours. The stallion followed and dropped to the ground only to rear again in a wild display of aggression. The stallion's uncontrolled threshing forced Horse to whip his head sideways to avoid a lethal kick. The stallion attacked with a sudden surge of confidence and bit into Horse's neck. Horse squealed in pain and a spray of red colored the air. Horse spun right, burning with rage, and delivered a series of rapid kicks at the air.

The stallion thinking his well-placed bite had defeated his challenger, rushed in. He charged with an open mouth just in time to receive a violent kick to the face. The crack of hooves on bone shattered the silence of the Comancheria and the stallion dropped to his knees. Horse, still angered over his bleeding neck, rammed the stallion with the top of his head. The violent impact once again rolled the stallion to his side.

Unsettled, the stallion tried to regain his feet by twisting his body frantically against the ground. Each time he would rise to his knees, Horse would rush forward and knock him down again. This went on for several minutes until the stallion simply rested on his belly, unwilling to try to rise anymore. Horse stared at the defeated stallion and backed several feet away.

The stallion surrendered, rose ungraciously and retreated slowly from the herd circle.

Victorious, but not yet finished, Horse rushed at and chased the once dominant stallion to the far edge of the herd's territory.

The herd broke its circle, and the lead mare moved out to greet Horse.

Parks lowered the field glasses and handed them to Free. "Appears Horse is the new stallion for that herd." Parks spat the chaw from his mouth, rolled over to his back and pulled his hat over his eyes.

Free looked over to Parks, “What are you doing?” he asked, exasperated.

“Might as well get some shut-eye, Free. There’s not much more we can do until those two get through honeymooning.”

CHAPTER 28

The Comancheria, Texas January 1869

Five days later, Parks and Free hid in a stand of mesquite and scrub oak trees. The dog sat fifty yards away and guarded the string of wild mustangs tied to the base of a large mesquite tree.

Parks issued a low warble-like whistle from the cover. Horse heard the unmistakable call from thirty yards away and headed toward the brush at a trot. The mare running close to his hip, slowed at the sound of the whistle and then stopped altogether. Horse looked back, nickered and bounced his head up and down as reassurance that it was safe to proceed. The mare lifted her ears, sniffed the air and then continued cautiously into the mesquites.

As the pair trotted into the scrub, Horse stopped and searched the low-lying mesquite branches for bean pods. The mare, still cautious, placed her nose to the ground and sniffed intently. From above, a shadow crossed her eyes and as she whirled to run, two loops of rope settled around her neck.

Free rode from his cover, jerked tight on his rope and then wrapped the lariat twice around his saddle horn. He clicked his tongue, pulled back hard on Spirit's reins and tightened the rope securely around the mare's neck. "Easy now, girl!" he hollered.

Parks jumped from behind a scrub oak and settled his rope just as the mare reared. Two turns of the rope bit deep into the palm of his hand. He pulled tight to sink the noose around the mare's neck and then hurriedly wrapped the rope around the oak's trunk. With the rope secure, Parks walked down the line toward the frightened mare. "Easy, girl," he whispered, avoiding eye contact.

Free continued to ease Spirit away from the mare. "You OK, Parks?" he shouted.

"I'm OK, just keep your line tight and we'll let her kick herself out. By my counting that gives us nineteen."

Free laughed, "I gotta hand it to you, Parks. I never thought we would be able to capture that herd in a week's time."

Parks fought to keep his hold on the rope line, "Don't thank me; thank Romeo over there."

An hour later, the mare had gentled and stood tied to a stringer with the rest of her herd. During the last week, Horse had managed to cut a lone mare from the herd and lead her into the brush where Parks and Free waited. The lead mare, the first to fall for the ruse, snickered continuously at Horse, obviously upset at his trickery.

Free laughed aloud and looked at Parks. "She appears to be giving Horse a piece of her mind."

"Looks like his honeymoon days are over."

Free smiled, nodded and then set his eyes intently on the horizon. "How far do you reckon it is to the Apache camp?"

Parks looked west. "I figure it's a two day ride to the Ghost Mountains. But a half-day's ride from here is the mail station at Barilla Springs. We can water there and maybe get some good information on where our Apache band is wintering."

Free clicked his tongue twice and spurred Spirit forward. "Let's get this herd moving then. Somewhere out there Clara's waiting for me."

The mail station at Barilla Springs lay twenty-eight miles northeast of Fort Davis. The flat land around the station was devoid of any brush or trees. Free and Parks arrived late in the afternoon, and each carried with them a fair portion of West Texas dust. The Kiowa dog cut a wide path to the north, preferring to keep a good distance from the station.

"A hot bath would sure feel good right now," Free remarked.

"I can tell you what little water they have in this country isn't *ever* used for bathing."

"Sounds uncivilized."

Parks chuckled, "I think the folks here consider that a compliment."

Three soldiers sat lazily outside the station but rose at the sight of the two cowboys leading a string of mustangs.

Parks rode up to the troopers and leaned forward in the saddle. "How are you gentlemen today?"

"Afternoon, sir,"

"Ninth Cavalry?" Free asked.

"Yes sir, Company E, sir. I'm Sergeant Jones."

Parks dismounted and looped Horse's reins over the makeshift hitching post. "Just you three here, Sergeant?"

"Yes sir. We're to meet up with more troopers tomorrow morning."

"Have you heard of any Apache causing trouble around here, Sergeant Jones?" Free stepped down from Spirit and tied his reins.

All three soldiers laughed aloud. "Only everyday, sir," the sergeant replied, "Our new commander has an expedition chasing the renegades in the Guadalupes right now."

Parks glanced over to Free. "In the Guadalupes?" he asked the soldier.

"Yes sir, Mescalero, sir."

Free dipped his bandana in a wooden water barrel and placed the rag against his face. "What about in the Ghost Mountains?"

"Oh, you won't find Apache there, sir. They believe spirits wander that mountain. The Apache call it, *chisos ni'*."

"What's that mean?" Free asked.

"The ghost ground. When the western wind whips through those mountain canyons it makes a whistling sound. The Indians say it is the cry of an Apache maiden. The legend is she jumped from the mountain rather then be abused by her white captors. The Apache believe she wanders the mountain calling to her village."

"And what do you think?" Parks asked.

"Me, sir? Well, let's just say I believe a man alone in that country at night can imagine and see lots of strange things."

Parks nodded and extended his hand to the sergeant, "I'm Parks Scott, and this here is Free Anderson."

"Sirs," the sergeant tipped his hat. "What brings you two to Barilla Springs?"

"My wife has been taken by Apache," Free said, sternly.

CHAPTER 29

Barilla Springs Country, Texas January 1869

Later, sitting next to a fire, surrounded by the desert darkness, Free relayed his story about Clara to the troopers.

Sergeant Jones shook his head. "We would gladly ride with you both, but we would need permission from our commander"

"That's not necessary, Sergeant. You have your own jobs to attend to. But we would be most appreciative to any information you can give us about where the Apache are wintering."

The sergeant scratched his head and stared into the glowing embers of the fire. "The band you're hunting may be Lipan or Mescalero or both. I can't say for sure, but if they're wintering down there, it would be south of the Ghost Mountains. There are a number of long, deep canyons in that country. You can spot them from a bend in the Rio Grande the Apache called *tuzigoot*."

"*Tuzigoot*?" Free asked.

"Yes sir, it means, crooked water, and if it were my wife, sir, that's where I would head."

The next day, a hundred miles out of Barilla Springs, the mustang herd pounded the dried chalk crust of the high desert into a fine powder. The prevailing southwest wind gusted across their faces and pushed the rising dust rapidly toward the northeast. The hostile land, sparsely dotted with white thorn and tarbush, seemed to be the perfect sanctuary for outcasts and hostiles.

In the late afternoon, Parks and Free stopped near a large dryfall of boulders along the base of the Ghost Mountains. The large, egg shaped rocks leaned against each other and formed a natural enclosure. The dog, not seen for much of the day, awaited the men on the northeast side of the dryfall where a small seep of water bubbled through a stand of winter grass.

Parks looked at the dog and grinned, "Did you find us some water, Dog?" He dismounted, dipped a handful of water from the seep and drank. "There's good water here, Free." He splashed water on his face, and then surveyed the surrounding country. "If we can find enough dead timber, we might be able to make a corral out of this dryfall stack."

Free stepped down from Spirit and touched one of the boulders. "These rocks are as big as this land," he said in awe.

"A man can't help but believe in someone larger than himself when he sees this land for the first time," Parks stated.

"Kind of peaceful out here." Free inhaled deeply and gazed at the mountains, "Once I get Clara back, this is the sort of land I could settle in."

"You aren't the first to make that statement." Parks grabbed the mustang string and led the ponies toward the seep. "After a month in this country though, they all run back to civilization."

Free looked puzzled. "Because of the Apache?" he asked.

"Because of the desolation. Loneliness will eat a man alive out here. Much as people hate to admit it, we humans seem to be herd animals too."

Before nightfall, the men built a gate of fir and pine deadfall hauled from the slopes of the Ghost Mountains. The nineteen mustangs, secured in the rock corral, fidgeted anxiously, stirred up by the small space. Spirit and Horse grazed in the shadows of the corral. Both lazily pulled up tender shoots of winter grasses near the water hole and nickered softly at the sounds of the mountain.

Parks leaned back against his saddle and held his bootless feet up to the fire. "Those mustangs should stay good for two or three days. They've had a long drink and seem to have eaten their fill in that winter grass stand. If our luck holds, I figure we ought to locate that Apache camp by tomorrow evening."

Free rubbed his hands over the fire and looked toward the darkness of the mountain. A ghostly cry drifted on the night breeze. "You hear that?" he shivered, suddenly chilled.

The dog raised his head and howled back at the ghostly sound.

"I think that sergeant knew what he was talking about, because that certainly sounds like a woman calling."

"Maybe, I'll reconsider settling in this country." Free scooted closer to the fire.

Parks pulled his feet away from the fire. "Free, there's a couple of things you need to know before we ride into that camp tomorrow."

Free sat upright. "What's that?"

"A man never knows the reception he will receive when riding into an Indian camp. You can bet they will see us long before we see them, and they will take special notice of Spirit's ear marking. If they are friendly with the Kiowa, we *might* be allowed into the camp unharmed. . ."

"And if they're not friendly with the Kiowa?"

"Then we best be ready to fight."

"I understand."

"And one more thing. . . ."

Free sensed something was troubling Parks. "What is it?"

"The Apache believe different than you or I. They think

stealing is part of being a man. If you can't protect your property, an Apache sees no problem with taking it."

"What are you getting at, Parks?"

"Just make sure you understand that in the Apache way of thinking, Clara belongs to them."

Free laid his hands on his thighs and pushed hard against his pants. "Well, that's crazy thinking. Clara doesn't belong to them! How could they believe such a thing!" he said angrily.

"We may all carry the look of men, Free, but it's our raising that sets us apart from one another. I'm telling you straight out that is what the Apache think. And if they see any sign of weakness from you, then our trading might go bad. Their culture doesn't respect a man who doesn't act like a warrior."

"That's my pregnant wife, Parks! I haven't seen her in almost a month, and now you're telling me if we do find her tomorrow, I need to look past her?"

"What I'm saying, Free, is we both want Clara back. But, if you ride into their camp at full chisel, it might cost both of us our lives. And getting ourselves killed isn't going to help Clara."

Free held his thoughts for several seconds and then looked up with an exacting steadiness. "I understand, Parks. I'll do what you say. But I won't be so obliged if any harm has been done to Clara or my child."

Parks saw something in his friend's face that went far beyond anger. He saw the look of a desperately reckless man who would fight for his family's safe return as long as he held breath in his lungs, no matter the price to be paid.

Suddenly, he dreaded the coming day and he hoped the Apache kept Clara hidden from Free.

CHAPTER 30

The Apache Winter Camp, Texas
January 1869

Clara worked a flesher made from the lower leg of a buffalo across the back of a hide. Next to her, Dayden worked feverishly rubbing brains into a freshly scraped pelt to keep the skin soft. It had been six days since she and the children arrived in the winter camp and the chores assigned her by the Apache squaws were now a part of her daily routine.

Her eyes darted around the camp surveying her canyon fortress. In spite of the realization that escape seemed hopeless, she nevertheless searched at every opportunity.

The older squaws kept a constant watch on her during the day. The same squaws berated Delshay with curses and hand gestures whenever he walked through the camp. Dayden said Delshay had broken with tradition by taking a captive over the age of twelve years, and he would endure such rebukes until Clara proved her value.

As she tirelessly scratched up the remaining tissue from the hide, she glanced toward the communal cooking pit. The five captured Mexican girls sat in a semi-circle around the fire mashing roasted sotol bulbs into a paste. Near the shallow water of the river, several Apache warriors patiently taught the two Mexican boys the art of shooting an Apache short bow.

"Cleyra." Dayden stood over Clara's back. "We go," she said and pointed toward the five girls.

Clara rose and followed Dayden toward the center of the camp where much of the tribe now gathered in a circle around the captured girls.

The oldest of the squaws, called Lupan, sat beside the first captured girl and began to stroke her long, coal black hair. The young girl presented a tight smile and offered her hair to Lupan, trying to be obedient because the squaw often beat the girls with a buffalo hair quirt.

Lupan deftly combed the girl's hair and chanted a rhythmic song with each stroke. The young girl listened for several minutes, lowered her head and relaxed. Lupan noticed the calm and rubbed the girl's upper arms while continuing to sing.

Then, without warning, Lupan twisted a handful of hair around her palm. The young girl's eyes widened in fear as Lupan violently jerked her head backwards.

Standing at the sotol pit, another squaw removed an orange-glowing iron from the embers and moved quickly toward Lupan. The young captive suddenly realized what was happening and fought to escape Lupan's clutches.

"What is going on?" Clara whispered, horrified.

"Shhh, Cleyra. The girls must be prepared for the traders."

The squaw with the hot iron grabbed the girl by the chin with a vice-like hold. Ignoring the child's struggle, she pushed the flat side of the brand onto the girl's left cheek.

The pitiful girl howled in agony. Before relaxing her grip, Lupan removed a large mesquite spine from her lap and punched the thorn through the girl's left ear lobe.

"The girl can now be traded," Dayden whispered to Clara.

Without a thought, Clara pushed her way through the crowd determined to stop Lupan. As she entered the circle, the front of her shirt dug deeply into her throat halting her movement. Confused, she turned and tried to free herself. To her shock, Delshay stood there and held a fistful of her shirt.

His eyes glowed dark with anger. With little concern for her pregnancy, he pushed her toward Dayden. "*Gunjule*!" he cautioned.

After each of the girl's faces had been branded and their ear's pierced, the squaws dragged them back to the chore of mashing sotol bulbs.

With the ceremony complete, Lupan rose and began to utter a series of loud cackles and howls. When she finished, the warriors near the river led the two captured boys into the ring. As the boys entered, the Apache became very excited and the noisy hum of chatter filled the air.

"Dayden, what are they doing?" Clara asked, anxiously.

"Lupan's son has gone to the spirit world. She has the right to choose her new son. The boys will fight so she can choose the one who is stronger."

Clara fought back the bile rising in her throat. She panted as her heart raced rapidly. She felt responsible for the ordeals facing the children and wondered why Free was taking so long to find her. *Please, Free. Please come soon*, she prayed.

The two captured boys stood in the ring and looked confused as Chan-deisi gestured for them to fight. Bewildered by his hand signals, both boys stood frozen, unsure of what to do. The frustration of the camp grew loud at the boys' reluctance and Clara feared what might happen if the boys did not obey.

Early in her life, she slaved on a farm near Victoria and at one time understood many Spanish phrases. Pressured to act quickly, she desperately tried to remember the Spanish word for "fight." "*Muchachos*!" she screamed over the crowd.

Both boys turned at the sound of their native tongue and looked her way.

Frantic, she held up her fists and shook them rapidly.

"*Combate*!" the word suddenly appeared to her, "*Ahora*!" she added.

The Apaches stared at Clara, quieted and then erupted into a loud roar as the boys grabbed each other and began to fight. The two released a ferocious rage that had smoldered during their captivity and began to rain a fury of fists and kicks upon each other. Like animals in the wild, the boys fought at a furious pace, urged on by the whoops of the Apache squaws.

After several minutes, the taller of the boys gained a dominant position and pinned his opponent to the ground. The boy landed a sharp punch and then began to strangle his foe.

Clara shuffled her feet in a rapid dance and tried to remain quiet. She watched the one boy turn ashen and unable to hold her tongue any longer, screamed out, "Help him!"

Delshay, standing in front of her, whirled and backhanded her across the face. A loud crack resonated around the circle and caused the Apache to glance up from the fight.

Clara stumbled backward and unable to regain her balance, fell hard to the ground. Angered, she looked up in defiance and swiped at the trickle of blood that formed on her mouth. Delshay's eyes seemed inflamed, and he held his outstretched hand above her, ready to strike again.

"Go ahead!" Clara screamed, "Hit me again! You are not a warrior, but a man who hits women!"

Delshay remained motionless, unsure of Clara's words.

Dayden rushed in and helped Clara regain her feet. "No Cleyra! No!" she screamed.

Clara held Dayden's hand and stared at the crowd. The boys had stopped their fighting and looked about their captors with heaving chests. Then both shook and cried uncontrollably as the rush of battle exited their bodies.

"*Hi-disho*!"

All of the Apache turned at the voice.

Standing outside the large tepee at the camp's center, a

stocky Apache dressed in a purple headband and a yellowed shirt held both hands skyward. "*Hi-disho*!" he repeated, calling an end to the encounter.

The tribe now directed their full attention on the civil-chief. Chanting in Apache, he pointed to Lupan and then to the boys. Next, he pointed all around the circle and rubbed his hands together.

The tribe erupted in laughter at his gestures. Finally, he pointed at Delshay, laughed loudly and spoke to Dayden. "Bring the buffalo woman to me!" he commanded.

The civil-chief of the Apache spread his arms across the interior of his tepee and offered Clara to sit.

"You have much courage, buffalo woman. That is a good sign. I am called Cochinay."

Clara nodded in respect. "Thank you, Cochinay. You speak very good English."

"*Ashoge*," Cochinay said, and then added, "Thank you. I learned English as a young boy from the border traders." Cochinay squatted and gracefully took a seat with crossed legs. "Tell me how it is you rode with the men who killed the Apache squaw in the great desert mountain?"

Clara reflected for a moment and then looked at the chief. "Cochinay, one month ago, the one man captured me and burned my house. I ran from this man and escaped, but he captured me again in the great white sands. I was a prisoner of those men like I am a prisoner of the Apache."

The chief studied Clara in silence. After a time he said, "Have you no man to protect you?"

Clara looked deep into Cochinay's eyes. "Yes. And he is coming here soon to find me."

Cochinay's face showed a quick flame of anger. "Any man who comes to the winter camp of the Apache uninvited must certainly die," he said.

CHAPTER 31

The Apacheria, Texas January 1869

The Kiowa dog sniffed at the ground with eager attention. He had remained in this one spot for well over five minutes trying to separate hundreds of different smells from one another.

Free stepped from Spirit and removed the tobacco pouch from around his neck. He waved the pouch back and forth under the dog's nose. "What do you smell? Do you smell Clara, boy?"

The dog set his nose against the pouch and began a series of rapid snorts. After another minute, he placed his nose back to the ground and then raced off to the northeast.

Parks reined Horse forward. A string of three ponies trailed behind him. He hoped to use the mustangs as a gift for the Apache leader. Parks watched the dog's movements and then glanced at Free. "Looks like he's back on the trail."

Free mounted Spirit and walked the mustang several paces behind the tracking dog. "Let's hope so."

The men had left their camp early in the morning and followed a javelina trail that cut through the overgrown sotol and yucca to the Rio Bravo. They traveled along the Texas side of the river for the better part of an hour before the dog picked up the first scent. But the Apache were smart; their trail crossed the river five times within a few miles, a strategy which confused the dog and made the Indian horses almost impossible to track.

Now back on the scent, the dog followed a wide bend in the river that emptied from mesquite and white thorn onto a large clearing at the mouth of a narrow canyon.

Free looked up the ravine and carefully studied the landscape. An enormous drift of sand climbed the northwest side of the canyon wall. The pile extended forty feet up the cliff walls. "This could be the canyon, Sergeant Jones spoke of."

Parks searched the top of the canyon walls for movement. He felt a hundred eyes on his back and was certain the Apache were here. Anxious, he calmly maneuvered Horse toward Free, even as his heart raced wildly. "We must be in the right spot. I can feel a dozen arrows pointed at me."

Free pushed his hat back and wiped his forehead with the sleeve of his shirt. "You too?"

"Yep." Parks continued to search the cliff walls. "I say we stop and let them come to us. We've lost the element of surprise, and we don't want to risk entering their camp uninvited."

"It sure is quiet all of a sudden." Free swiveled in the saddle and looked in all directions trying to locate the dog.

"Too quiet."

"Dog!" Free called out, "Com'on, Dog! Get back here!"

The only sound in the canyon was that of the river rolling at their backs. Parks reached up and removed his bandana. He tied the blue cloth around the barrel of his Winchester and then placed the butt of the rifle on his thigh. "Can't hurt to let them know we came to talk," he said.

"I wonder where that dog's gone." Free lifted the Henry to his chest as a precaution and then from the corner of his eye, caught movement near the sand drift. He tossed a glance toward the pile just as the dog streaked into view. The dog sprinted full chisel toward Free leaving a spray of sand in his wake.

Behind him, a band of ten Apache followed in single file.

The Apache never hurried their ponies, and they rode within several feet of Free and Parks. The lead rider, dressed in a long yellow shirt and wide purple headband, looked at the men and studied their faces. “To steal a Tejano’s horse brings great honor to the Apache,” he said, proudly.

“We come in peace,” Free answered.

The leader turned to his warriors and spoke Apache. The braves all broke out in laughter.

“We don’t need the Tejano’s peace,” the lead rider replied.

“We offer the Apache chief a gift.” Parks held up the mustang string.

The lead rider tightened his jaw, raised his hand, and quickly made a fist. “We will take the ponies!” Then his face relaxed as if bored with the men before him. “*Zaastee*,” he said, calmly.

The Apache braves all drew arrows and notched them into their bowstrings.

“Stay calm,” Parks whispered.

One of the braves moved close to Free and held a drawn arrow inches from his heart. The Kiowa dog stood underneath Spirit and uttered a low warning growl to the brave.

“Quiet, Dog,” Parks uttered, and then to Free, “Don’t move a muscle.”

After several seconds, the leader moved beside the brave and pushed the warrior’s bow downward. “OK, Tejano, you give us the ponies.”

Free, Parks and the Kiowa dog sat in the soft soil of the river’s bank and under guard of seven Apache braves. To their north, the leader and the remaining braves rode the wild ponies in and out of the canyon mouth, whooping and hollering, pleased at the mustangs speed.

"Why do they keep calling us Tejano’s?" Free asked, puzzled.

Parks watched the Apache riding skills in fascination and then replied, "The Apache make no distinction between Mexicans and Texians. To them, we are all just intruders on their land."

Free nodded and asked, "How'd you know they weren't going to kill us back there?"

"I didn't. But, I did remember Colonel Ford saying an Apache gets excited when he orders a death. That chief was calm when he told his braves to kill us. I reckoned they were just trying to test our courage."

The Apache chief rode back to Free and Parks flashing a broad smile. He dismounted and sat across from the men. "Good Apache horses, Tejano," he laughed. "*Ashoge*! I am Cochinay."

"I am Free."

"You ride a horse marked by the Kiowa, Free."

"Yes, a gift from White Horse."

Cochinay spoke to his warriors in Apache. The braves raised their bows at White Horse's name. "We know of this Kiowa. He refuses to sign peace treaties with the whites."

"And he is a friend," Free said.

"All right, friend of the Kiowa," Cochinay looked at both men, "What do the Tejano's want from the Apache?"

"We wish to trade with Cochinay."

Cochinay straightened, "We have your ponies." he spread his hands away from his body. "What else do you have?"

Parks stared into Cochinay's eyes. "We have many more horses."

Cochinay looked all around the river. "Where? Where are these horses?"

Parks smiled. "Hidden. Hidden far from here. Where only the Tejanos can find them."

"All right, Tejano." Cochinay studied his opponents carefully. "You are smart. We trade our best buffalo skins for your horses."

Parks moved closer. "We have no use for hides," he shrugged.

Cochinay spoke in Apache and then held both hands palms up. "All the Apache have for trade is buffalo skins."

"What about hostages?" Free asked.

Cochinay appeared confused by the question. He looked back and spoke to one of his braves. The brave answered rapidly and pointed back toward the canyon. Cochinay shook his head as if remembering and then said, "Yes, we have five Mexican girls waiting for the traders. Are you the traders for these girls?"

"You don't have a wo . . ."

Parks tapped Free on the shoulder and interrupted his question. "Yes, Cochinay." Parks said, "We are here to trade for the Mexican girls."

Cochinay grinned. "Good, Tejanos. You get your ponies and meet us here one day from now, and we will take you to the girls."

Parks and Free pushed the mustangs at a harsh pace on the return to the Ghost Mountains. The Kiowa dog lagged behind, distracted by a new scent on the trail.

They rode in silence, knowing it was important to reach the camp before dark. This would be a long night as they prepared for tomorrow's trade at the Apache camp.

In the late afternoon and under the falling shadows of the mountain, they reached the rock corral.

"We best take care of these horses." Free stepped down from Spirit and uncinched his saddle.

"I'll drag up some wood with Horse before I wipe him down," Parks said.

Free nodded and tossed his saddle next to last night's fire. He removed a rag from his pack and wiped the sweat from Spirit. "Good boy," he patted the mustang's neck and glanced into the corral. The mustangs fidgeted about and nickered quietly. "I don't blame you," he spoke to the lead mare; "I hate being locked up too." He quickly counted the herd and then removed the water bladder from his saddle. "I'll rustle us up some water," he spoke aloud.

As he rounded the large, corner boulder of the corral, a shadow crossed his path, and he instinctively reached for his Colt.

"Hold it right there,"Mr. Colored Man."

Free froze and stared down the working end of a Winchester rifle. He raised his hands slowly and stared at the man holding the gun.

"I bet you weren't expecting to see me again, were you?" Nathan Polk lowered the Winchester to Free's belly. Behind him stood two ruffians.

"Hello, Polk."

"You might want to meet these two fellas as well." Polk pushed the barrel of the Winchester farther into Free's belly. "The one goes by Ward and the other Charlie." Polk showed a mouthful of yellowed teeth. "Ward and Charlie Fischer. And they are the kin to those two boys you plugged at *Agua de Mesteño*."

CHAPTER 32

The Apacheria, Texas January 1869

"Where's that mutt of yours?" Polk moved cautiously behind Free, not wanting a repeat of their last encounter. He leaned against the large corner boulder of the corral, peeked around the rock and scanned the vacant campsite. "And where's your friend? I owe them both a little something." He looked toward the darken shadows of the mountain and then out into the desert.

"I'm alone, Polk."

Ward Fischer, a powerful looking man, walked straight up to Free. Both men stood the same height. "Is that a fact?" he said, gruffly and then swung a hard fist into Free's jaw. Ward pulled his hand back and shook it several times. "You were right about him being an uppity colored, Nathan."

Free dipped slightly at the blow and then stood back straight. He rubbed his jaw and stared hard at Ward. "I'm alone," he repeated.

Charlie Fischer, younger and smaller than Ward, sized up Free and then turned to the others. "Let's string him up right now!" he yelled, "For what he did to Isham and Coy!"

"Hold your tongue, Charlie." Ward cautioned his brother, as he removed Free's Colt from its holster. "We don't know where his partner is, and I sure as heck don't want him knowing where we are. Get this one tied up and sit him on the ground." Ward glanced back to Polk. "See anything, Nathan?"

"Nothing. The shadows off that mountain makes it impossible to see a darn thing."

Ward moved next to Polk. "Help Charlie get the colored tied up before he tries something stupid."

Charlie hurried to his horse and pulled a length of rawhide from his saddle horn. "Bring him over here, Nathan."

Polk shoved the Winchester into Free's back and prodded him forward. "Get over there, Mr. Colored Man," he ordered.

Free walked toward Charlie as instructed, *I can't be messing with these three tonight*, he thought. *And I can't help Clara if I let them tie me up*. He glanced at the darkening sky and figured now was as good a time as any to act. He strode three more steps, halted in midstride and reeled quickly to his left, pushing Polk's rifle skyward as he turned.

Polk jumped in surprise as Free raced by him. Free's quickness caught him off guard, and he yelled, "He's loose, Ward! Stop him!"

Free lowered his head and accelerated toward Ward. He knew if Polk got a shot off before he rounded the corner, he was a dead man.

"What?" Ward Fischer turned, surprised, and tried to see what was causing all the commotion.

Free flew by Ward and landed a well-placed elbow to the ruffian's nose as he went. "Parks! Free screamed into the darkness, "It's Polk and two more! Take cover!"

Ward grabbed his nose with both hands and howled in anger. "My nose! He broke my nose!"

Charlie hurried over to his brother and hollered, "Don't just stand there, Polk! Shoot him!"

Polk ran past the boulder into the open and began shooting blindly into the night.

"Stop it!" Ward slapped at Polk's arm. "Stop it! You're just wasting bullets, you danged fool!"

Free sprinted through the camp and snatched the Henry rifle from his saddle ring. He continued full bore for the heavy brush at the base of the mountain. "Parks!" he shouted, "I'm coming your way!" He raced through a clump of cedar, ducking as the heavy branches slapped at his face. Fifty yards into the brush, a hand reached out and stopped his progress. "Parks?" he whispered.

"Yep."

"Thank, God!" Free exhaled and bent over to catch his wind.

"It's Polk?" Parks asked.

Free nodded his head in frustration, "How could he have tracked us here?"

Parks gazed toward the corral, searching for movement by the men. "I don't think he followed us, Free."

"What do you mean?"

"I have a feeling that those three are headed to the Apache winter camp."

The realization of Parks' words hit Free like a kick to the stomach. "They're the border traders?"

Parks shrugged. "They probably trade with the Apache several times a year. I reckon they're trading repeaters with Cochinay for captured children."

Free grimaced. "If that's right, then they're probably sitting on a whole load of ammo."

Parks rolled his Colt's cylinder and checked his load. "Most likely," he said.

From across the way, Ward called into the darkness. "Hey, Mr. Colored Man! You broke my nose! Now, I owe you for more than just Isham and Coy!"

Free searched the darkness for any moving shadows and then whispered to Parks. "We have to do deal with these traders tonight. If we don't show in the morning, Cochinay may not receive us again."

"Hey, Mr. Colored Man!" Ward called out again, "What are you doing with all the mustangs? You weren't planning on heading to Cochinay's camp to trade them, were you?"

"What do you want, Ward?" Free hollered.

A blare of gunfire erupted at the sound of Free's voice. As the shots quieted, Ward called out again, "Did we hit you, Mr. Colored Man?"

Free frowned. "Com'on, Ward!" he shouted across the camp, "Let's work out a deal. I only want to get my wife back from the Apache! That's all I'm aiming to do!"

Laughter erupted from the corral. "Why do you want her back, Mr. Colored Man? She's soiled goods now. I probably could trade her for a broke-down mule, but that's about it!"

Free turned to Parks. "Those boys are . . . ." He stared into the spot where he had last seen his friend and realized Parks had disappeared. "Parks," he whispered, "Parks? Where are you?" He scanned the cedars, but it was hopeless in the total blackness. He looked back toward the corral and tried once more to negotiate with the Fischers. "Ward, there must be something we can work out!"

The flash of gunfire erupted again. Free fell to his stomach and lay flat as cedar limbs danced in the air above him.

"How about now, Mr. Colored Man? Did we hit ya yet?" Ward yelled, "If we didn't, we've got lots of ammo over here to try with!"

Free backed up several feet and took cover behind a larger cedar. "Think about it, Ward! I'll give you whatever you want!"

"We'll think it over while we're reloading!" Ward laughed, crazily. "And then we'll get you an answer!"

"I tell you what, Ward! Let me get my wife away from the Apache, and I'll surrender to you! When I'm sure she's safe, you can kill me or hang me or whatever you want to do!"

The night erupted once more in the flash of gunfire. As the trader's guns emptied, a solitary shot rang out in the darkness from above the corral. Then all went quiet, except for a groan and the sound of Ward cussing, "I'm hit, Charlie! They shot me good."

"Ward!" Charlie hollered, "Ward! Hang on! I'm coming!"

The corral area held quiet for several minutes, and then Charlie screamed in rage, "You killed Ward! You killed Ward!" and then he yelled, "He must be behind us, Polk!"

Free inched forward on his belly, Henry in hand, and stared into the darkness. He was afraid to talk any further as Parks was somewhere behind the two remaining men.

Suddenly, six shots rang out and the whole of the desert floor streaked with running shadows.

"Free!" Parks shouted from above the corral. "They've cut the mustangs loose!"

"There!" Charlie shouted and fired in the direction of Parks' voice.

Free rose and ran unthinking toward the corral. He waved his hat in vain and tried to turn the horses around. But the panicked herd stampeded past him. As the last of the mares roared into the night, he knew they would not stop for miles. Free dropped to his knees and slammed the Henry to the ground in despair. "What have I done, Clara? What have I done?" he cried.

Near the corral, another lone shot rang out, and the moan of a man falling hard sounded across the desert.

Free lifted his head at the gun's report. "Parks!" he screamed, "Are you OK?" Frantic, he scanned the night and saw a dark shadow to his left.

"I don't know, Mr. Colored Man," the shadow answered.

Free froze and felt Nathan Polk push the barrel of the Winchester against his temple.

"But, no matter what else happens tonight, I'm going to kill you." Polk levered the Winchester.

Free stared at the dark figure unbowed and waited for his bullet.

CHAPTER 33

The Apacheria, Texas January 1869

The pungent odor of intruders drifted along the javelina trail and alerted the Kiowa dog to danger. He lifted his nose to the wind and then raced in silence toward the source of the smell. He locked on the scent and in seconds was racing toward a dark form standing on the desert floor.

The dog reached the figure quickly and recognized the smell as that of the trader. He left his feet, hit the man with full force and knocked him to the ground.

Overpowered, Nathan Polk stumbled, squeezed the Winchester's trigger and fired a bullet into the ground near Free.

The dog bounced off Polk and hit the ground violently. He rolled head over tail and landed on his back several feet away. Growling, he scrambled to his feet and raced back toward Polk, barking in a wild rage.

Polk gained his balance and turned to Free. He raised the rifle when the dog struck him again. Polk staggered and toppled over on his back.

In seconds, the dog straddled Polk and clamped his powerful jaws on the trader's throat.

Free struggled to his feet and ran to the dog. "Good, Dog!" he yelled, and then directed his attention to Polk, "Are you crazy, Polk! I out to . . . ."

"Free!" A shout broke through the darkness.

Free jerked his head up and looked in the direction of the voice. "Parks!" he cried out, "Where are you?" He tossed a quick glance at the dog and Polk, and then raced toward his friend.

At first light, Free surveyed the carnage. Parks rested against his saddle with a bullet hole on his left side, just below the ribcage. Free knelt and removed Parks' bandage. Blood still seeped from the wound, but it was a through and through hole. "You're lucky, Parks." he patted his friend's chest softly.

"It was a lucky shot in the dark." Parks grimaced.

Free spread yucca paste on a piece of wool rag. "This should keep the poison out." He placed the bandage on the wound.

"Did we lose all the mustangs?" Parks asked.

"Every last one of them. And the trader's horses too. And the repeaters and the ammo. They're all probably a hundred miles away by now." Free stared blankly across the desert.

"And Polk?"

Free glanced at the dog, lying quietly nearby. "Dog took care of Polk."

"I'll get up shortly," Parks said, "We'll fix this somehow, Free. We can still get Clara back safely."

Free gazed at the three bodies lying motionless in the morning sun. "You're not fit to ride anywhere, Parks. Just lie still for now. I'll figure this out."

"But, I know we . . . ." Parks stopped and then bolted upright. "I've got it. We'll challenge Cochinay to a race."

"What?" Free asked, "What are you saying?"

"That's it." Parks became lost in his thoughts and then said, "The Apache love sport, Free. The ultimate honor to an Apache is winning a challenge. Cochinay won't refuse."

"So they would rather race against us than kill us?"

"Not exactly, but they would accept the challenge of a race if the loser had to pay with something precious."

"But, we don't have anything valuable right now, Parks. We barely have enough ammunition to load our Colts again."

"Oh, we've got something Cochinay wants . . ."

Free hesitated and then asked, ". . . and that is?"

"Our scalps."

CHAPTER 34

Cañon de Sierra Carmel, January Texas 1869

Free sat on Horse and stared anxiously at Cochinay and his warriors. Parks had insisted he ride Horse to the Apache powwow this morning, "*He's faster than any Apache pony, and you know he can outpace Spirit at any distance. It's your best chance of getting Clara back,*" Parks had said.

"Tejano, where is your friend?" Cochinay finally spoke and broke the uneasy silence. "He is not hiding above?" Cochinay scanned the high cliffs that surrounded them.

"No, Cochinay, men ambushed us last night and shot my friend."

"Ah, this is dangerous country, Tejano. Many men die in the Apache land." Cochinay looked past Free. "And the horses?"

"The traders ran off our horses." Free sat tall in the saddle and tried to disguise his fear. His heart pounded loudly in his chest as he waited for Cochinay's reaction.

Cochinay shrugged. "Then you have nothing to trade?"

"Not horses," Free replied.

Cochinay looked back and spoke to his braves. The Apache warriors listened, nodded and then turned their horses back toward the canyon mouth.

"Good-bye, Tejano." Cochinay said, "Be glad Cochinay is kind and lets you leave with your life."

"Wait!" Free yelled.

Cochinay continued to walk his horse away, but turned and glanced back over his shoulder.

"Surely, the Apache are not afraid to listen to the Tejano?"

Cochinay frowned and then pulled reins on his pony. "Be careful of your tongue, Tejano." He spoke with authority, "It fights only with words, no match for an Apache blade." Cochinay pulled a long bladed flint knife from his sash.

"My tongue only offers a better trade, Cochinay."

Cochinay stared deep into Free's eyes. "What is better than horses, Tejano?"

"Sport."

Cochinay relaxed and laughed. "Sport?" Cochinay tapped at his temple several times. "Maybe the Tejano is *loco*."

"A challenge, Cochinay. I have always heard the Apache love a challenge."

Cochinay spoke aloud in Apache. The braves listened to their chief and then laughed loudly.

"A challenge, Cochinay, with my scalp as the prize." Free removed his hat and showed the Apache a thick head of hair.

Cochinay studied Free with a careful intent.

"Cochinay can take your hair now if he wants."

"But that wouldn't show the Apache courage. No, to beat the Tejano at a race and then take his scalp is the Apache way," Free offered.

"How do you know the Apache way, Tejano?" Cochinay flipped his hand out as if to dismiss Free.

"A race as far as Cochinay chooses."

Cochinay smiled. "An Apache race, Tejano?"

Free nodded. "Yes, an Apache race. My horse against the best Apache horse."

Cochinay grinned broadly. "All right, Tejano. We race the Apache way. And if the Apache win, we take the Tejano's life, his horse and his hair."

"Done," Free replied without hesitation. "And if the Tejano

wins, he gets to keep his life and his hair, and his scalp, and the . . . ."

"Done," Cochinay interrupted.

". . . the hostages," Free finished.

Cochinay nodded his acceptance.

"Cochinay," Free continued, "*all* the hostages."

Cochinay looked at Free with understanding. "The buffalo woman, she is yours, Tejano?"

Free answered deliberately. "She is my wife, Cochinay, and I aim to take her home."

CHAPTER 35

The Apache Winter Camp, Texas January 1869

Free stood, surrounded by Apache squaws. The women slapped at his body with horsetail quirts and chattered relentlessly at his presence. Free withstood the assault with a calm indifference and stared expressionless at his tormentors.

Cochinay took a position next to Free and raised his hands high into the air. The squaws stopped their ceremony at his signal and backed away. Cochinay spoke rapidly in Apache and then pointed to Free. The whole village burst out in fervor at his words. Ecstatic, the squaws immediately formed two lines and began to chant at one another. One line would yell, "*Chelee*!" and the other side would respond with, "*Gah*!" The back and forth kept building in volume until the whole tribe engaged in the taunting.

"Do you understand, Tejano?" Cochinay asked, smiling.

"I can't say that I do." Free listened to Cochinay's explanation, but his thoughts were preoccupied with Clara. He scanned the camp diligently for any sight of her.

"One side calls "horse." The other side calls "rabbit." It is our sport. Rabbit and horse."

"I still don't understand." Free gazed at Cochinay, confused.

"The Tejano asked to race the Apache way. So, first you run like a rabbit up the cliff to your horse and then the horses race. That is the sport, Tejano."

Free swallowed hard and wondered what he had gotten himself into. "What about my wife?" he asked.

"The Tejano will see the buffalo woman if he wins the race." Cochinay scanned the crowd and motioned with his hand toward the assembled warriors. A muscular Apache brave stepped forward at Cochinay's signal and strode over to Free.

Cochinay took the brave's hand and placed it atop Free's. "Tejano," Cochinay spoke loudly, "this is your opponent, Delshay. He is the warrior married to the buffalo woman."

Free glared at Delshay, drew a deep breath and tried to keep his composure.

As the ceremony quieted, Cochinay pointed at the back canyon wall. A half mile up the cliff walls, an Apache warrior stood and held the reins to two horses in his hands.

"Tejano! You will race up the cliff to your horse. On top, you will ride to the spot where the sun rises each day. There you will find an Apache arrow buried into the stalk of a sotol bush. The arrow bears a purple ribbon and the man who brings the ribbon back to me is the champion."

"Is that all?" Free asked above the noise.

"No, Tejano." Cochinay slapped his thighs with both hands. A brave from the crowd emerged and handed the chief two bows and eight arrows.

"*Netdahe*!" Cochinay yelled out, "Each man can kill the other at any time, but be careful, for each man gets but four arrows."

Free exhaled loudly.

"What is wrong, Tejano? Is this not the race you chose?" Cochinay mocked, "The Apache way."

Delshay reached for his bow and shook the weapon at Free. "*Gusano*!" he screamed.

The squaws erupted in laughter. Free looked at Cochinay perplexed.

"He calls you a worm." Cochinay joined in the laughter.

Free smiled and grabbed for his bow. "Tell him, I will wait for his return when I race back first."

Cochinay turned to Delshay and relayed Free's words. Delshay eyes darkened in anger. "*Gusano*!" he repeated.

Cochinay grabbed both men's hands. "When I release your hand, Tejano, the race is on."

Free looked over to Delshay and slipped the bow over his neck and shoulder. Delshay glared back and shook his arrows at Free.

In the building noise, Free felt Cochinay release his hand; he glanced at Delshay and then sprang forward in an explosive burst of speed. The squaws roared loudly as both men raced neck in neck for the back wall and soon the whole village joined in and ran behind them.

After thirty yards, Free felt his muscles relax and he eased slightly ahead of Delshay. He pumped his hands furiously as he sprinted for the trail, now visible at the base of the cliff.

Losing ground, Delshay drifted slightly behind Free. The Apache brave carried the four-foot bow in his right hand and before they reached the trail, Delshay pushed the bow in between Free's feet.

Free tumbled and fell to his knees. Delshay sidestepped him and pushed hard on Free's left shoulder as he raced by. Free crumpled and rolled across the rocky ground of the canyon floor. As his body came to a stop, the snap of wood cracked loudly and a stabbing pain burned across his back. Free rose and saw a long sliver of wood embedded in his shoulder. He struggled to his feet, reached back and with a piercing scream jerked the broken point from his flesh. Maddened, he slammed the splintered bow to the ground and then rushed furiously after Delshay.

Free hurried up the tortuous Apache trail and winced in pain with each footfall. Delshay was already a third of the way up the canyon and moving quickly. Free glanced to both sides as he ran, looking for a shorter path to the canyon rim. To his right, he noticed a worn animal trail and without hesitation bounded onto the track. The path was laden with scrub that grabbed at his legs as he tried to move forward. Determined, he swung at the vegetation with the four arrows he carried and in minutes began to gain ground. Delshay continued to move confidently up the winding path to the rim of the canyon and his waiting steed.

Fifty feet ahead and on a dead run, Delshay stopped and loaded an arrow into his bow. He turned and pulled back on the bowstring determined to kill or wound his opponent.

Free watched Delshay string an arrow and dropped forward. He flattened against the ground as the arrow whooshed by and pierced the ground beside him. He waited for several more seconds, pushed himself up and began once more the furious sprint to Horse.

As he crested the canyon rim, he saw Delshay mounted and racing away. *Com'on, Free!* he scolded, *Run!* He raced with arrows in hand the twenty yards to Horse and pounced into the saddle with a mighty leap. Horse jumped as Free's weight settled on his back, and the mustang roared after the Apache pony. Sensing the urgency, Horse laid his ears back and burst forward in an explosion of speed that soon propelled him even with Delshay.

Free maneuvered Horse to Delshay's right side, wanting to make sure the Apache brave could not easily draw an arrow on him. Delshay recognized the ploy, slowed slightly and dropped behind, hoping to get a shot at Free's back. Free watched Delshay lose ground and reined Horse hard in an evasive measure.

Delshay shouted in anger as Free thwarted his tactic. He glanced over and then rammed his pony into Horse. As the animals bumped one another, Delshay lunged from his horse and knocked Free from the saddle.

Both men bounced on the hard surface of the upper rim and rolled apart. Delshay gained his feet first and looked about for his bow. Free shook his head and scrambled to his feet. He yelled and raced for Delshay with a raised hand. He rushed three steps and stopped abruptly. He stared at his empty hand and then swung his gaze over to Delshay.

The Apache brave locked eyes with Free and then glanced down. Embedded in his right side were four arrows. Delshay groaned in pain and then dropped to his knees.

Free hesitated and watched as Delshay desperately tried to push the arrow points through his body. He stood transfixed and then blinked as he regained his senses. He whistled for Horse, re-mounted and raced off in search of the purple ribbon.

Free led Delshay's horse into the Indian camp. The waiting line of squaws stood silent as he rode past. He reined Horse to a stop outside of Cochinay's tepee. The squaws then rushed to Delshay's pony and pulled the injured warrior to the ground. Several braves joined in and carried their badly wounded comrade to his tepee.

"The Tejano is weak," Cochinay walked up to Free. "Delshay would have left the Tejano to die."

Free handed the purple ribbon to Cochinay and then dismounted. "Where is my wife?" he asked, defiantly.

Cochinay nodded and gazed toward Delshay's tepee. He shouted loudly in Apache and then slapped both thighs. Free looked in the direction of his shouts and watched as children began to emerge from the tepee flap.

Without caution, Free started for the tepee, first walking and then running, oblivious of the Apache around him. He counted as seven children emerged, and then he saw Clara.

He muttered her name and then ran for her, hollering louder with each step. "Clara!"

Clara looked in the direction of her name and saw Free. Unable to restrain herself, she unleashed a river of tears and ran screaming his name. "Free!"

The two rushed into each other's arms and embraced in a long hug.

"Free! You don't know how I've prayed to see you. I thought—."

"Shh." Free looked deep into her eyes, "I'm here now and that's all that matters." He glanced at her stomach and then back into her eyes.

Clara nodded, understanding his unspoken question. "We're going to have a baby, Free."

Free held her tight and swung her around. As they twirled, Free noticed the captive children around them. Each child carried a look of concern. He looked at them all and said, "We're going to take you home, every one of you, today!"

The children stood expressionless.

"They don't understand English, Free." Clara wiped away her tears and smiled at the children. "*Vamanos a la casa*," she said.

Free, Clara and the seven children walked back to Cochinay. From above the canyon entrance, a loud whistle sounded. Cochinay tossed a quick glance at his lookout and then back to Free. He yelled at several braves in great urgency and signaled for them to mount up. The warriors quickly raced for their ponies and prepared to ride from the camp. And then the unnerving bark of a dog carried down the ravine and echoed around the canyon walls.

Free grinned. "It's OK, Cochinay. It's the other Tejano and the dog."

Cochinay held his hand up and halted the braves. From around the last bend leading to the camp, Parks and Dog appeared. Parks, atop Spirit, led the trader's packhorses into the camp.

Later, Parks, Free and Clara rode across the shallow crossing of the Rio Bravo. The children each shared a packhorse, and one rode behind Parks.

"I still can't believe you were able to round up those packhorses with a bullet hole in your side, Parks."

"Well, Dog was aggravating me more than the bullet hole and the horses didn't really run that far. I suspect the load of repeaters and ammo on their backs caused them to rethink that."

"And I can't believe you brought the repeaters to the Apache."

"Oh, I wouldn't worry too much about that, Free. Those rifles don't shoot very well with fouled firing pins. And the ammo is hidden in the Ghost Mountains. I don't think we need worry about the Apache wandering around there."

Clara leaned against Free's back and smiled at Parks. "It feels so good to see you both again."

Parks tipped his hat at Clara, "My sentiments exactly, Clara." he said, and then looked over to Free. "What's next, cowboy?"

Free glanced around at the Mexican captives and smiled at each one. "We best get these children back to their folks," he said. "Then you and me have a house and corral that need re-building."

ACKNOWLEDGEMENTS

Silent gratitude isn't much use to anyone.

—G.B. Stern

Many thanks to:

Mindy Reed, Fred Tarpley, Weldon L. Edwards, and Stephanie Barko.

RIDE THE DESPERATE TRAIL

GLOSSARY

Slang:

Among the willows — Hiding from the law   pg. 93

Beating the devil around the stump — Wasting time pg. 64

Bangtail — Mustang   pg. 64

Bite the ground — Dead   pg. 65

Big Fifty — A fifty caliber rifle   pg. 67

Full chisel — Full speed   pg. 152

Lucifer — A sulphur match   pg. 74

Top Notch — A man's scalp   pg. 85

Comanche Phrases and Names

Cuhtz baví — Buffalo brother   pg. 53

Haa — Yes   pg. 54

Marʉaweeka — Hello   pg. 53

Mow-way — Push aside or shaking hand   pg. 54

Ʉra — Thank you   pg. 54

Spanish Phrases and Names:

Ahora — Now   pg. 155

Agua de Mesteño — Stray water   pg. 42

Bebidas y Mecancías — Drinks and merchandise pg. 9

Fiesta — Party pg. 9

Camino del muerte — Road of death pg. 79

Cañon de Sierra Carmel — Canyon of the Carmel Mountains pg. 135

Combate — Fight pg. 155

El Paso del Rio del Norte — early name for the city of Juarez pg. 125

Muchachos — Boys pg. 155

Ojo Aridó — Dry eye pg. 117

Vamanos a la casa — Let's go to the house pg. 180

Apache Phrases:

Ashoge — Thank you pg. 157

Chan-deisi — Broken Nose pg. 125

Chelee — Horse pg. 175

Cochinay — Yellow Thunder pg. 157

Dayden — Little girl pg. 138

Delshay — Walking Bear pg. 125

Gah — Rabbit pg. 175

Gunjule — Be good pg. 127

Hi-disho — It is finished pg. 156

Lupan — Gray Fox pg. 154

Netdahe — Death to all pg. 176

Nzhoo — Very good pg. 129

Tuzigoot — Crooked water pg. 149

Zaastee — Kill pg. 160

RIDE THE DESPERATE TRAIL

Discussion Questions

What is major theme of the novel?

The novel has an underlying minor theme. What do you think the minor theme of the novel is?

The author raises the question of social and cultural indoctrination in the novel. What is social and cultural indoctrination?

What indoctrination formed Tig Hardy's view of others?

Do any of the other characters have a chance to escape their indoctrinations? What traits do these characters possess that allows them to escape?

What do you think McCaslin's character represents in society?

Do you think all cultures feel they alone possess the correct worldview?

How do cultures arrive at this belief?

Is war a result of social and cultural indoctrination?

The book's plot takes the reader through many twists and turns. What are the major obstacles Free must overcome in his quest to rescue Clara?

Do you think Free escapes his times?

Do you think Clara's character escapes her times? What role did society dictate for frontier women?

The book contains Native Americans characters. Do you think the Native American characters are forced to play out societal roles?

Do societal dictated roles conflict with individual freedoms? Explain.

AMBUSH AT MUSTANG CANYON: THE END OF THE TRAIL

A Free Anderson-Parks Scott Novel

(978-0-9788422-0-0)

By Mike Kearby

Available Fall of 2007

Turn the page for a preview